William Shakespeare

The Comedy of Twelfth Night

What you will

William Shakespeare

The Comedy of Twelfth Night
What you will

ISBN/EAN: 9783337255862

Printed in Europe, USA, Canada, Australia, Japan

Cover: Foto ©Andreas Hilbeck / pixelio.de

More available books at **www.hansebooks.com**

THE COMEDY

OF

TWELFTH NIGHT

OR, WHAT YOU WILL

BY

WILLIAM SHAKESPEARE

NEW YORK ·:· CINCINNATI ·:· CHICAGO

AMERICAN BOOK COMPANY

1892

INTRODUCTION.

[Abridged from Professor Dowden's Sketch of William Shakespeare.]

WARWICKSHIRE has been named by Shakespeare's contemporary and fellow-poet, Michael Drayton, "the heart of England." The country around Stratford presents the perfection of quiet English scenery. It is remarkable for its wealth of lovely wild flowers, for its deep meadows on each side of the tranquil Avon, and for its rich, sweet woodlands. The town itself, in Shakespeare's time, numbered about 1400 inhabitants, —a town of scattered timber houses, possessing two chief buildings: the stately church by the riverside; and the Guildhall, where companies of players would at times perform, when the corporation secured their services. Flood and fire were the chief dangers of the town. The quiet river often rose angrily in autumn, and left disease behind it. The plague, in its course, did not turn aside from Stratford. Here, and probably in a low-ceiled room of a house in Henley Street, William Shakespeare was born, in April, 1564,— upon what day we cannot be certain, but upon the 26th he was baptized; and there is a tradition that the day of his death (April 23) was the anniversary of his birthday.

John Shakespeare, father of the future dramatist, was a prosperous burgess of Stratford. He made and sold gloves, farmed land, and, though he knew not how to write his name, became an important public person of the town, tasting ale for his fellow-

3

burgesses, keeping the Queen's peace, imposing fines upon offend-
ers, rising in course of time to the honorable posts of chamberlain, alderman, and high bailiff.   He married, in 1557, Mary
Arden, daughter of his landlord, who had died about a year before, leaving Mary a considerable piece of landed property in
possession (including a farm at Ashbies), and one much more
valuable in reversion.   The Ardens had been Warwickshire gentry
since before the Conquest, and two of the family had held places
of distinction in the household of Henry VII.   The first child,
and the second, of John and Mary Shakespeare, were girls, who
died while infants; the third — their first-born son — was to live,
in spite of the plague which desolated Stratford during the year
of his birth, and was to write the plays and poems that we know.

   To the Free Grammar School of Stratford William Shakespeare
was sent, we may be sure, to learn what neither his father nor
his mother could teach.   There he was taught not only English,
but some Latin, and perhaps a little Greek.   Afterwards, perhaps during his London life, Shakespeare seems to have learned
something of French, and possibly also of Italian.   In the first
year in which Shakespeare could have been admitted to the Free
Grammar School, his father became chief alderman of Stratford.
The corporation seem to have welcomed the players who occa-
sionally visited the town.   The boy, his father's eldest son, may
have been taken to see the entertainments in the Guildhall.   In
the summer of 1575 Queen Elizabeth made her famous visit to
Kenilworth, and was entertained by Leicester with splendid and
varied ceremonies and spectacles.   From Stratford it is only a
few hours' walk to Kenilworth : Shakespeare's father might ride
across with the boy before him.

   In November, 1582, the Bishop of Worcester granted a license for the marriage of William Shakespeare and Anne Hathaway. Anne was the daughter of Richard Hathaway, a substantial yeoman living at Shottery, a beautiful hamlet hardly one mile distant from Stratford. For four or five years he resided in Stratford, and in 1585 became the father of twins, Hamnet and Judith, named after his friends Hamnet Sadler and his wife. Most probably during the poet's London life, Anne, with his children, staid in Stratford. It was in Stratford, in 1596, that Hamnet, his only son, was buried. Though Shakespeare chose to leave his wife and children in the country, while he himself was toiling in the great city, a tradition records that he paid a yearly visit to his home. There is no doubt that he toiled with the purpose of returning, as he actually did, to his native town, there, with his family, to spend the later years of his life.

The immediate cause of Shakespeare's departure from Stratford is thus told circumstantially by Rowe, his first biographer: " He had, by a misfortune common enough to young fellows, fallen into ill company; and amongst them, some that made a frequent practice of deer-stealing engaged him more than once in robbing a park that belonged to Sir Thomas Lucy of Charlcote, near Stratford. For this he was prosecuted by that gentleman, as he thought, somewhat too severely; and, in order to revenge the ill usage, he made a ballad upon him. And though this, probably the first, essay of his poetry be lost, yet it is said to have been so very bitter, that it redoubled the prosecution against him to that degree, that he was obliged to leave his business and family in Warwickshire for some time, and shelter himself in London." Part of this story is probably incorrect, but it undoubtedly has a foundation of fact.

From the baptism of his twins in February, 1584, nothing is

heard of Shakespeare until he is spoken of in 1592 as a suc-
cessful actor and author. The " Queen's Players " came to
Stratford in 1587. Then perhaps it was that Shakespeare decided
to leave his native town, and seek his fortune in London. The
first certain reference to Shakespeare which has been discovered
is that of the dramatist Robert Greene, in his " Greenes Groatsworth of Wit bought with a Million of Repentance,"—a pamphlet written by its unhappy author upon his death-bed, and
published immediately after Greene's death by his executor,
Henry Chettle. Here the dying playwright, addressing three
of his fellow-authors, warns them against putting any trust
in players: "Yes, trust them not : for there is an upstart
Crow, beautified with our feathers, that with his tygers heart
wrapt in a players hide, supposes he is as well able to bumbast
out a blanke verse as the best of you: and being an absolute
Johannes factotum, is in his owne conceit the onely SHAKE-
SCENE in a country." We have evidence here that before
Greene's death the players had been turning from him to a
rival poet who was also an actor, who could write a swelling
blank verse like Marlowe, who turned his hand to everything, and
made himself useful in many ways to his company.

Some three months later, in December, 1592, a pamphlet by
Henry Chettle appeared, entitled " Kind-Harts Dream." It
seems that Marlowe and Shakespeare took offense at passages
in " Greenes Groatsworth " referring to them. Chettle declares
that as for one of them (Marlowe), while he reverences his
learning, he has nothing to answer for, and cares not ever to
make his acquaintance. To Shakespeare he offers a liberal
apology. "The other [*Shakespeare*] whome at that time I
did not so much spare as since I wish I had . . . I am as

sory as if the originall fault had beene my fault, because my selfe have seene his demeanor no lesse civill, than he exelent in the qualitie he professes; besides, divers of worship have reported his uprightnes of dealing, which argues his honesty, and his facetious [*felicitous*] grace in writting, that aprooves his art." The word "qualitie," it should be noted, was used in Shakespeare's time with special reference to the actor's profession; so that we here possess testimony to Shakespeare's worth as a man, to his excellence in his profession, and to the friends and fame he had already acquired as a writer.

The first mention we possess of Shakespeare by name, after his arrival in London, occurs in the accounts of the treasurer of the chamber, from which we learn that he appeared twice with Burbage as a member of the lord chamberlain's company, before Queen Elizabeth, in Christmas time, 1593. He was now rapidly producing his historical plays and earlier comedies, and was gathering that wealth which he meant should release him from the servitude of his profession. He had planned to return in due time to Stratford, and to live there as a gentleman. In 1596 John Shakespeare applied for a grant of coat armor, and in the following year the grant was made by the Garter King-of-Arms. But if Shakespeare hoped to found a family, that hope received a blow; and the father's heart was wounded by the death, in 1596, of Hamnet, his only son. Still he pursued his plan, and looked forward to Stratford as his home. An attempt was made at this time by John Shakespeare and his wife to recover Ashbies, probably without success. In 1597, William Shakespeare bought, for £60, New Place, a goodly dwelling in his native town.

In 1598 most remarkable testimony to the high position occupied by Shakespeare as a dramatist and as a narrative and lyrical poet is given in the "Wit's Treasury" by Francis Meres, master of arts. The passage in which Meres enumerates twelve of Shakespeare's plays is of the utmost importance in guiding us towards a true chronology of his works; it must also be observed that Meres makes mention of Shakespeare's "Sugred sonnets among his private friends." The earliest editions of plays by Shakespeare belong to this period. In 1597 were printed "Richard II.," "Richard III.," and "Romeo and Juliet." Others speedily followed. It is clear that in several instances the copies were obtained surreptitiously; and, to gain a sale for plays by other authors, unscrupulous printers now placed the popular name of Shakespeare upon the title-page. In 1599 a volume of poems, entitled "The Passionate Pilgrim," was published, and its authorship ascribed to Shakespeare. Jaggard, the publisher, had got hold of a few short pieces of Shakespeare's, and added to these liberally from other quarters. We know, on the testimony of Heywood, that Shakespeare, upon occasion of a subsequent edition containing poems falsely ascribed to him, was seriously offended.

In 1601 died at Stratford the poet's father, John Shakespeare. Still his son pursued his plan of providing himself with a substantial independence and a home. The play of "Hamlet" is entered in Stationers' Register in 1602; and in the same year the creator of "Hamlet" was living in no dream-world, but was taking practical possession of this solid earth; purchasing in May, for £320, one hundred and seven acres in the parish of Old Stratford (his brother Gilbert receiving the conveyance for him), and later in the year (the author of "Hamlet" being now "William Shakespeare, *Gentleman*") a second and smaller property. His largest purchase was that of the unexpired term of a lease of the tithes of Stratford, Old Stratford, Bishopton, and Welcombe.

This he acquired in July, 1605, for the sum of £440. But, although now styled "gentleman, of Stratford-on-Avon," he had not yet left London, nor abandoned his profession. Elizabeth died in 1603. It was noticed at the time that Shakespeare lamented the Queen in no ode or elegy. In May arrived at London her successor, James I.; and within a few days after his arrival a warrant was issued, licensing the theatrical company to which Shakespeare belonged. His name appears second in the list of players contained in the warrant. Ben Jonson's "Sejanus" was first acted in the same year, 1603, and the name of Shakespeare occupies a place in the list of actors. We know nothing of his having acted at a later date than this; but whether he ceased to appear upon the stage about 1604, or continued to act for several years later, we cannot say.

Between the years 1610 and 1612 we have reason to suppose that Shakespeare returned for good to his Stratford home. The change was great from the streets of London, the noisy theaters, the brilliant "wit-combats" at the Mermaid Tavern, to the peaceful retreat, the wife whom he had loved as a boy, his children and their little girl, by this time running about and talking, and encircling these the quiet fields and hills and brimming river. Still he retained an interest in London. In the following year, 1613, the Globe Theater was destroyed by fire, and probably manuscripts of Shakespeare's plays perished on that occasion. Fire again may have alarmed, if it did not injure, Shakespeare, in 1614; for in that year a great conflagration took place at Stratford, fifty-four houses being burned down. At the same time a project was put forward for the inclosing of some common lands near Stratford. It touched Shakespeare's interests, and would have been an injury to the poor: Shakespeare resisted the scheme, declaring that he was not able to bear the inclosing of Welcombe.

On Feb. 10, 1616, Shakespeare's younger daughter, Judith, now aged thirty-one, was married to Thomas Quiney, a vintner of Stratford, whose father — a friend of the poet — had been high bailiff of the town.   On the 25th of the next month he executed his will, which in January had been drawn, and in another month the world had lost Shakespeare.   He died April 23, 1616. Shakespeare was buried in the parish church at Stratford.   Within a few years after his death a bust of the poet was erected in the church.   The face was probably modeled from a cast taken after death.   It was originally colored, — the eyes hazel, the hair and beard auburn.   This and the portrait which is prefixed to the First Folio, 1623, are the only certain likenesses of Shakespeare which remain to us.   That known as the "Chandos portrait," though differing in some important particulars from the other portraits, has by many persons been considered genuine; and there exists a death-mask — named, from a supposed former owner, the "Kesselstadt death-mask" — which bears the date 1616, and which may be the original cast from the dead poet's face.   It exhibits a head of remarkable proportions, and a face of great power and refinement.   The grave in the parish church at Stratford is covered by a flat stone, bearing an inscription attributed to Shakespeare himself: —

> " Good frend, for Jesus' sake forbeare
> To digg the dust enclosed heare:
> Blest be the man that spares thes stones,
> And curst be he that moves my bones."

A comedy acted at Siena in 1531, and printed at Venice six years later, bears the title " Gl'Ingannati," or, "The Deceived."

The analysis of the story is this: "Fabritio and Lelia, brother and sister, are separated at the sack of Rome, in 1527. Lelia is carried to Modena, where resides Flaminio, to whom she had formerly been attached. Lelia disguises herself as a boy, and enters his service. Flaminio had forgotten Lelia, and was a suitor to Isabella, a Modenese lady. Lelia, in her male attire, is employed in love embassies from Flaminio to Isabella. Isabella is insensible to the importunities of Flaminio, but conceives a violent passion for Lelia, mistaking her for a man. In the third act Fabritio arrives at Modena, where mistakes arise owing to the close resemblance there is between Fabritio and his sister in her male attire. Ultimately recognitions take place; the affections of Isabella are easily transferred from Lelia to Fabritio, and Flaminio takes to his bosom the affectionate and faithful Lelia."

This is in outline the story of "Twelfth Night," and from the Italian comedy Shakespeare certainly derived his plot. "But it by no means follows," says Dyce, "that the foreign originals were used by Shakespeare; and, indeed, I suspect that his knowledge of Italian was small. Much of the lighter literature of his time — many a printed tale and many a manuscript play — has long ago perished; and among them may have been some piece translated or imitated from the Italian, which supplied him with materials for the serious parts of 'Twelfth Night;'" for it is to be noted that the comic characters of the underplot — Sir Toby, Sir Andrew, the Clown, Maria, and Malvolio himself — are entirely of Shakespeare's creation, as are, of course, all of the beauties and the poetry of the piece.

Two facts fix the date of this play at about 1599 or 1600. The name of "Twelfth Night" is not found in Meres's list of 1598, and it could hardly, therefore, have been printed or acted before that. The fact on the other side is this: Among the Harleian Manuscripts in the British Museum is a small volume containing, among other things, the diary of a member of the Middle Temple from January, 1601, to April, 1603. The writer of this diary has been identified with one John Manningham, who was entered at the Middle Temple, March 16, 1597. The entry which concerns us reads,—

"Febr. 1601. At our feast wee had a play called Twelve night or what you will. much like the comedy of errores or Menechmi in Plautus, but most like and neere to that in Italian called Inganni a good practise in it to make the steward beleeve his Lady widdowe was in Love with him by counterfayting a letter, as from his Lady, in generall termes, telling him what shee liked best in him, and prescribing his gesture in smiling his apparaile &c. And then when he came to practise making him beleeve they tooke him to be mad."

This entry of Manningham's is quite sufficient to identify the play which was acted in the Middle Temple Hall at the Readers' Feast, 1601–02, with the "Twelfth Night" of Shakespeare.

Various conjectures have been made as to the reason of the name given to this comedy; but the most probable one seems to be that Shakespeare considered this comedy suitable for representation on Twelfth Night, which was then always kept in England with amusements and festivities. The second title of "What You Will" was probably added by Shakespeare to show that if "Twelfth Night" was not a good enough name, people could choose for themselves, and call it by whatever name they preferred (compare the title "As You Like It"). This was to a certain extent done: for some twenty years after its first production the play was called "Malvolio."

TWELFTH NIGHT;

OR, WHAT YOU WILL.

PERSONS OF THE PLAY.

ORSINO, Duke of Illyria.
SEBASTIAN, *brother to Viola.*
ANTONIO, *a sea captain, friend to Sebastian.*
A Sea Captain, *friend to Viola.*
VALENTINE, } *gentlemen attending on*
CURIO, } *the Duke.*
SIR TOBY BELCH, *uncle to Olivia.*
SIR ANDREW AGUECHEEK.

MALVOLIO, *steward to Olivia.*
FABIAN, }
FESTE, *a Clown,* } *servants to Olivia.*
OLIVIA.
VIOLA.
MARIA, *Olivia's woman.*
Lords, Priests, Sailors, Officers, Musicians, and other Attendants.

SCENE: *A city in Illyria, and the seacoast near it.*

ACT I.

SCENE I. *The Duke's Palace.*

Enter DUKE, CURIO, *and other* Lords; Musicians *attending.*

Duke. If music be the food of love, play on;
Give me excess of it, that, surfeiting,
The appetite may sicken, and so die.
That strain again! it had a dying fall:[1]
O, it came o'er my ear like the sweet south,
That breathes upon a bank of violets,
Stealing and giving odor! Enough; no more:

[1] "A dying fall," i.e., it died away softly.

13

"Tis not so sweet now as it was before.
O spirit of love! how quick and fresh art thou,
That, notwithstanding thy capacity
Receiveth as the sea, nought enters there,
Of what validity[1] and pitch soe'er,
But falls into abatement and low price,
Even in a minute: so full of shapes is fancy[2]
That it alone is high fantastical.[3]

   Curio. Will you go hunt, my lord?
   Duke.   What, Curio?
   Curio. The hart.
   Duke. Why, so I do, the noblest that I have:
O, when mine eyes did see Olivia first,
Methought she purg'd the air of pestilence!
That instant was I turn'd into a hart;[4]
And my desires, like fell and cruel hounds,
E'er since pursue me.

Enter VALENTINE.

                How now! what news from her?
   Valentine. So please my lord, I might not be admitted;
But from her handmaid do return this answer:
The element itself, till seven years' heat,[5]
Shall not behold her face at ample view;
But, like a cloistress, she will veiled walk
And water once a day her chamber round
With eye-offending brine: all this to season
A brother's dead love, which she would keep fresh
And lasting in her sad remembrance.

---

1 Value.   2 Love.
3 " High fantastical," i.e., in the highest degree imaginative.
4 In reference to one of the fables of Ovid's Metamorphoses, in which Actæon, while hunting, having discovered Diana bathing, is by her trans-formed to a hart, and, being pursued by his own hounds, is devoured by them.
5 " Seven years' heat," i.e., seven years' heat has passed.

Duke. O, she that hath a heart of that fine frame
To pay this debt of love but to a brother,
How will she love, when the rich golden shaft
Hath kill'd the flock of all affections else
That live in her; when liver, brain and heart,
These sovereign thrones, her sweet perfections,[1]
Are all supplied and fill'd with one self king!
Away before me to sweet beds of flowers:
Love-thoughts lie rich when canopied with bowers.   [*Exeunt.*

SCENE II.   *The Seacoast.*

Enter VIOLA, *a* Captain, *and* Sailors.

Viola. What country, friends, is this?
Captain. This is Illyria, lady.
Viola. And what should I do in Illyria?
My brother he is in Elysium.
Perchance he is not drown'd: what think you, sailors?
Captain. It is perchance that you yourself were sav'd.
Viola. O my poor brother! and so perchance may he be.
Captain. True, madam: and, to comfort you with chance,
Assure yourself, after our ship did split,
When you and those poor number saved with you
Hung on our driving[2] boat, I saw your brother,
Most provident in peril, bind himself,
Courage and hope both teaching him the practice,
To a strong mast that liv'd upon the sea;
Where, like Arion[3] on the dolphin's back,

---

[1] " Her sweet perfections " represent the judgments, passions, and senti-
ments, of which it was supposed the liver, brain, and heart were respectively
the seats.

[2] Drifting.

[3] " Arion on the dolphin's," etc.   Arion was a famous musician of
Methymna in the Island of Lesbos.   He visited Italy, and obtained great
wealth by his profession.   Some time after, he wished to return to his native

I saw him hold acquaintance with the waves
So long as I could see.

Viola. For saying so, there's gold:
Mine own escape unfoldeth to my hope,
Whereto thy speech serves for authority,
The like of him. Know'st thou this country?

Captain. Ay, madam, well; for I was bred and born
Not three hours' travel from this very place.

Viola. Who governs here?

Captain. A noble duke, in nature as in name.

Viola. What is his name?

Captain. Orsino.

Viola. Orsino! I have heard my father name him:
He was a bachelor then.

Captain. And so is now, or was so very late;
For but a month ago I went from hence,
And then 'twas fresh in murmur,— as, you know,
What great ones do the less will prattle of,—
That he did seek the love of fair Olivia.

Viola. What's she?

Captain. A virtuous maid, the daughter of a count
That died some twelvemonth since, then leaving her
In the protection of his son, her brother,
Who shortly also died: for whose dear love,
They say, she hath abjur'd the company
And sight of men.

Viola.   O that I serv'd that lady
And might not be delivered to the world,

country; and the sailors of the ship on which he was embarked conspired to murder him and obtain the riches he was carrying to Lesbos. Arion begged that before being put to death he might be permitted to play some melodious tune. As soon as he had finished, he threw himself into the sea. A number of dolphins had been attracted round the vessel by the sweetness of his music, and it is said he was borne on the back of one of them in safety to Tænarus.

Till I had made mine own occasion mellow,
What my estate is!¹

Captain.   That were hard to compass;
Because she will admit no kind of suit,
No, not the duke's.

Viola. There is a fair behavior in thee, captain;
And though that nature with a beauteous wall
Doth oft close in pollution, yet of thee
I will believe thou hast a mind that suits
With this thy fair and outward character.
I prithee, and I'll pay thee bounteously,
Conceal me what I am, and be my aid
For such disguise as haply shall become
The form of my intent. I'll serve this duke:
Thou shalt present me as a singer to him:
It may be worth thy pains; for I can sing
And speak to him in many sorts of music
That will allow² me very worth his service.
What else may hap to time I will commit;
Only shape thou thy silence to my wit.

Captain. Be you his singer, and your mute I'll be:
When my tongue blabs, then let mine eyes not see.

Viola. I thank thee: lead me on.   [*Exeunt.*

SCENE III. *Olivia's House.*

Enter SIR TOBY BELCH *and* MARIA.

Sir Toby. What a plague means my niece, to take the death
of her brother thus? I am sure care's an enemy to life.

Maria. By my troth, Sir Toby, you must come in earlier o'
nights: your cousin,³ my lady, takes great exceptions to your ill
hours.

---

¹ "And might not be," etc., i.e., and that my identity might not be made
public until I find occasion to reveal it.   ² Approve.

³ "Cousin" was loosely used to designate any kindred not in the first
degree, — niece, nephew, uncle, grandchild, etc.

2

Sir Toby. Why, let her except, before excepted.[1]

Maria. Ay, but you must confine yourself within the modest limits of order.

Sir Toby. Confine! I'll confine myself no finer than I am: these clothes are good enough to drink in; and so be these boots too; an they be not, let them hang themselves in their own straps.

Maria. That quaffing and drinking will undo you: I heard my lady talk of it yesterday; and of a foolish knight that you brought in one night here to be her wooer.

Sir Toby. Who, Sir Andrew Aguecheek?

Maria. Ay, he.

Sir Toby. He's as tall[2] a man as any's in Illyria.

Maria. What's that to the purpose?

Sir Toby. Why, he has three thousand ducats a year.

Maria. Ay, but he'll have but a year in all these ducats: he's a very fool and a prodigal.

Sir Toby. Fie, that you'll say so! he plays o' the viol-de-gamboys,[3] and speaks three or four languages word for word without book, and hath all the good gifts of nature.

Maria. He hath indeed, almost natural:[4] for besides that he's a fool, he's a great quarreler; and but that he hath the gift of a coward to allay the gust he hath in quarreling, 'tis thought among the prudent he would quickly have the gift of a grave.

Sir Toby. By this hand, they are scoundrels and substractors that say so of him. Who are they?

Maria. They that add, moreover, he's drunk nightly in your company.

Sir Toby. With drinking healths to my niece: I'll drink to her

---

[1] " Except before excepted " was an old law phrase which Sir Toby uses ludicrously enough, and intentionally without meaning.

[2] Able.

[3] Sir Toby's corruption of " viol-da-gamba," a musical instrument like the violoncello.

[4] Maria puns on the word in its sense of " fool " or " idiot."

as long as there is a passage in my throat and drink in Illyria: he's a coward and a coistril[1] that will not drink to my niece till his brains turn o' the toe like a parish-top.[2] What, wench? Castiliano vulgo![3] for here comes Sir Andrew Agueface.

Enter SIR ANDREW AGUECHEEK.

Sir Andrew. Sir Toby Belch! how now, Sir Toby Belch!

Sir Toby. Sweet Sir Andrew!

Sir Andrew. Bless you, fair shrew.

Maria. And you too, sir.

Sir Toby. Accost, Sir Andrew, accost.

Sir Andrew. What's that?

Sir Toby. My niece's chambermaid.

Sir Andrew. Good Mistress Accost, I desire better acquaintance.

Maria. My name is Mary, sir.

Sir Andrew. Good Mistress Mary Accost—

Sir Toby. You mistake, knight: "accost" is front her, address her, woo her.

Sir Andrew. By my troth, I would not woo her in this company. Is that the meaning of "accost"?

Maria. Fare you well, gentlemen.

Sir Toby. An thou let part[4] so, Sir Andrew, would thou mightst never draw sword again.

Sir Andrew. An you part so, mistress, I would I might never draw sword again. Fair lady, do you think you have fools in hand?

Maria. Sir, I have not you by the hand.

---

[1] A contemptible fellow.

[2] In Shakespeare's time "a large top was kept in every village to be used in frosty weather, that the peasants might be kept warm by exercise, and out of mischief while they could not work."

[3] Probably Sir Toby's mistake for the Italian *Castiliano volto*, i.e., put on a Castilian face, that is, look grave and solemn.

[4] "Let part," i.e., let her depart.

Sir Andrew. Marry,[1] but you shall have; and here's my hand.

Maria. Now, sir, "thought is free:" I pray you, bring your hand to the buttery-bar[2] and let it drink.

Sir Andrew. Wherefore, sweet-heart? what's your metaphor?

Maria. It's dry, sir.

Sir Andrew. Why, I think so: I am not such an ass but I can keep my hand dry. But what's your jest?

Maria. A dry jest, sir.

Sir Andrew. Are you full of them?

Maria. Ay, sir, I have them at my fingers' ends: marry, now I let go your hand, I am barren. [*Exit.*

Sir Toby. O knight, thou lack'st a cup of canary:[3] when did I see thee so put down?

Sir Andrew. Never in your life, I think; unless you see canary put me down. Methinks sometimes I have no more wit than a Christian or an ordinary man has: but I am a great eater of beef, and I believe that does harm to my wit.

Sir Toby. No question.

Sir Andrew. An I thought that, I'ld forswear it. I'll ride home to-morrow, Sir Toby.

Sir Toby. Pourquoi,[4] my dear knight?

Sir Andrew. What is "pourquoi"? do or not do? I would I had bestowed that time in the tongues that I have in fencing, dancing and bear-baiting: O, had I but followed the arts!

Sir Toby. Then hadst thou had an excellent head of hair.[5]

Sir Andrew. Why, would that have mended my hair?

---

[1] This petty oath, so frequent in old plays, is a corruption of "By the Virgin Mary," and was used in avoidance of the statute against profane swearing.

[2] The "buttery" was a room in which provisions and liquors were kept; the "bar," the opening through which they were passed.

[3] A sweet wine of the Canary Islands.

[4] For what, why.

[5] Sir Toby puns on "tongues" and "tongs" (curling-tongs for the hair). The words were formerly pronounced more nearly alike than at the present time.

Sir Toby. Past question; for thou seest it will not curl by nature.

Sir Andrew. But it becomes me well enough, does't not?

Sir Toby. Excellent; it hangs like flax on a distaff.

Sir Andrew. Faith, I'll home to-morrow, Sir Toby: your niece will not be seen; or if she be, it's four to one she'll none of me: the count himself here hard by woos her.

Sir Toby. She'll none o' the count: she'll not match above her degree, neither in estate, years, nor wit; I have heard her swear't. Tut, there's life in't, man.

Sir Andrew. I'll stay a month longer. I am a fellow o' the strangest mind i' the world; I delight in masques and revels sometimes altogether.

Sir Toby. Art thou good at these kickshawses,[1] knight?

Sir Andrew. As any man in Illyria, whatsoever he be, under the degree of my betters; and yet I will not compare with an old man.

Sir Toby. What is thy excellence in a galliard,[2] knight?

Sir Andrew. Faith, I can cut a caper.

Sir Toby. And I can cut the mutton to't.[3]

Sir Andrew. And I think I have the back-trick simply as strong as any man in Illyria.

Sir Toby. Wherefore are these things hid? wherefore have these gifts a curtain before 'em? are they like to take dust, like Mistress Mall's[4] picture? why dost thou not go to church in a galliard and come home in a coranto?[2] My very walk should be a jig. What dost thou mean? Is it a world to hide virtues in? I did think, by the excellent constitution of thy leg, it was form'd under the star of a galliard.

---

[1] Kickshaws; trifles.   [2] A lively Spanish dance.

[3] We learn from the knight's quibble on the word, that " capers " were served with mutton as long ago as Shakespeare's day at least.

[4] It is probable this means simply a lady's picture; " as we say ' Master Tom ' or ' Master Jack ' to designate no particular individual, but young gentlemen generally."

Sir Andrew. Ay, 'tis strong, and it does indifferent well in a flame-color'd stock.[1]   Shall we set about some revels?

Sir Toby. What shall we do else? were we not born under Taurus?[2]

Sir Andrew. Taurus!   That's sides and heart.

Sir Toby. No, sir; it is legs and thighs.   Let me see thee caper: ha! higher: ha, ha! excellent!   [*Exeunt.*

SCENE IV.   *The Duke's Palace.*

Enter VALENTINE, *and* VIOLA *in man's attire.*

Valentine. If the duke continue these favors towards you, Cesario, you are like to be much advanc'd: he hath known you but three days, and already you are no stranger.

Viola. You either fear his humor or my negligence, that you call in question the continuance of his love: is he inconstant, sir, in his favors?

Valentine. No, believe me.

Viola. I thank you.   Here comes the count.

Enter DUKE, CURIO, *and* Attendants.

Duke. Who saw Cesario, ho?

Viola. On your attendance, my lord; here.

Duke. Stand you a while aloof.   Cesario,
Thou know'st no less but[3] all; I have unclasp'd
To thee the book even of my secret soul:
Therefore, good youth, address thy gait unto her;
Be not denied access, stand at her doors,

1 Stocking.
2 An allusion to the astrology of the almanac, which refers the affections of particular parts of the body to the predominance of the constellations of the zodiac.   Both Sir Toby and Sir Andrew are wrong, as Taurus was supposed to govern the neck and the throat.
3 Than.

And tell them, there thy fixed foot shall grow
Till thou have audience.
   Viola.   Sure, my noble lord,
If she be so abandon'd to her sorrow
As it is spoke, she never will admit me.
   Duke. Be clamorous and leap all civil bounds
Rather than make unprofited[1] return.
   Viola. Say I do speak with her, my lord, what then?
   Duke. O, then unfold the passion of my love,
Surprise her with discourse of my dear faith:
It shall become thee well to act my woes;
She will attend it better in thy youth
Than in a nuncio's of more grave aspect.
   Viola. I think not so, my lord.
   Duke.   Dear lad, believe it;
For they shall yet belie thy happy years,
That say thou art a man: Diana's lip
Is not more smooth and rubious;[2] thy small pipe
Is as the maiden's organ, shrill in sound,
And all is semblative a woman's part.
I know thy constellation is right apt
For this affair. Some four or five attend him;
All, if you will; for I myself am best
When least in company. Prosper well in this,
And thou shalt live as freely as thy lord,
To call his fortunes thine.
   Viola.   I'll do my best
To woo your lady: [*Aside*] yet, a barful strife!
Whoe'er I woo, myself would be his wife.   [*Exeunt.*

---

[1] Unprofitable.   [2] Red like a ruby.

Scene V.   *Olivia's House.*

Enter MARIA *and* CLOWN.

Maria. Nay, either tell me where thou hast been, or I will not open my lips so wide as a bristle may enter in way of thy excuse: my lady will hang thee for thy absence.

Clown. Let her hang me: he that is well hang'd in this world needs to fear no colors.[1]

Maria. Make that good.

Clown. He shall see none to fear.

Maria. A good lenten[2] answer: I can tell thee where that saying was born, of "I fear no colors."

Clown. Where, good Mistress Mary?

Maria. In the wars; and that may you be bold to say in your foolery.

Clown. Well, God give them wisdom that have it; and those that are fools, let them use their talents.

Maria. Yet you will be hang'd for being so long absent; or, to be turn'd away, is not that as good as a hanging to you?

Clown. Many a good hanging prevents a bad marriage; and, for turning away, let summer bear it out.[3]

Maria. You are resolute, then?

Clown. Not so, neither; but I am resolv'd on two points.

Maria. That if one break, the other will hold; or, if both break, your gaskins[4] fall.

Clown. Apt, in good faith; very apt. Well, go thy way; if

---

1 " Fear no colors," i.e., fear no enemy. We still use " colors " for " flag " or " standard." It was a proverbial saying, and is often met with in dramas of the time.

2 Meager, like the fare in Lent.

3 " Let summer," etc., i.e., he could get on well enough if he were dismissed in summer.

4 A kind of trousers. The tags with which they were fastened to the doublet were also called " points," and Maria puns on the word in this sense.

Sir Toby would leave drinking, thou wert as witty a piece of Eve's flesh as any in Illyria.

Maria. Peace, you rogue, no more o' that.   Here comes my lady: make your excuse wisely, you were best.   [*Exit.*

Clown. Wit, an't be thy will, put me into good fooling! Those wits, that think they have thee, do very oft prove fools; and I, that am sure I lack thee, may pass for a wise man: for what says Quinapalus?[1] "Better a witty fool than a foolish wit."

Enter Lady OLIVIA *with* MALVOLIO.

God bless thee, lady! ·

Olivia. Take the fool away.

Clown. Do you not hear, fellows?   Take away the lady.

Olivia. Go to, you're a dry fool; I'll no more of you: besides, you grow dishonest.

Clown. Two faults, madonna,[2] that drink and good counsel will amend: for give the dry fool drink, then is the fool not dry: bid the dishonest man mend himself; if he mend, he is no longer dishonest; if he cannot, let the botcher[3] mend him.   Anything that's mended is but patch'd: virtue that transgresses is but patch'd with sin; and sin that amends is but patch'd with virtue. If that this simple syllogism will serve, so; if it will not, what remedy?   The lady bade take away the fool; therefore, I say again, take her away.

Olivia. Sir, I bade them take away you.

Clown. Misprision in the highest degree!   Lady, cucullus non facit monachum;[4] that's as much to say as I wear not

---

[1] The clown invents a philosopher as authority for his own aphorism. We hear of him again as having exercised his inventive genius in producing Pigrogromitus, the Vapians, and "the Equinoctial of Queubus," for the entertainment of Sir Andrew.

[2] My lady.

[3] A patcher of old garments.

[4] "Cucullus non facit monachum," i.e., the cowl does not make the monk.

motley [1] in my brain.   Good madonra, give me leave to prove
you a fool.

Olivia. Can you do it?

Clown. Dexteriously,[2] good madonna.

Olivia. Make your proof.

Clown. I must catechize you for it, madonna: good my
mouse [3] of virtue, answer me.

Olivia. Well, sir, for want of other idleness, I'll bide your
proof.

Clown. Good madonna, why mourn'st thou?

Olivia. Good fool, for my brother's death.

Clown. I think his soul is in hell, madonna.

Olivia. I know his soul is in heaven, fool.

Clown. The more fool, madonna, to mourn for your brother's
soul being in heaven.   Take away the fool, gentlemen.

Olivia. What think you of this fool, Malvolio? doth he not
mend?

Malvolio. Yes, and shall do till the pangs of death shake
him: infirmity, that decays the wise, doth ever make the better
fool.

Clown. God send you, sir, a speedy infirmity, for the better
increasing your folly!   Sir Toby will be sworn that I am no
fox; but he will not pass his word for twopence that you are no
fool.

Olivia. How say you to that, Malvolio?

Malvolio. I marvel your ladyship takes delight in such a
barren rascal: I saw him put down the other day with [4] an ordinary fool that has no more brain than a stone.   Look you now,
he's out of his guard already; unless you laugh and minister
occasion to him, he is gagg'd.   I protest, I take these wise men,

---

[1] Consisting of different colors.   The customary dress of the fool or
jester was party-colored.

[2] An intentional corruption, no doubt.

[3] A familiar term of endearment.

[4] By.

that crow so at these set kind of fools, no better than the fools' zanies.[1]

Olivia. O, you are sick of self-love, Malvolio, and taste with a distemper'd appetite. To be generous, guiltless and of free disposition, is to take those things for bird-bolts [2] that you deem cannon-bullets: there is no slander in an allow'd fool, though he do nothing but rail; nor no railing in a known discreet man, though he do nothing but reprove.

Clown. Now Mercury endue thee with leasing,[3] for thou speak'st well of fools!

Reënter MARIA.

Maria. Madam, there is at the gate a young gentleman much desires to speak with you.

Olivia. From the Count Orsino, is it?

Maria. I know not, madam: 'tis a fair young man, and well attended.

Olivia. Who of my people hold him in delay?

Maria. Sir Toby, madam, your kinsman.

Olivia. Fetch him off, I pray you; he speaks nothing but madman: fie on him! [*Exit Maria.*] Go you, Malvolio: if it be a suit from the count, I am sick, or not at home; what you will, to dismiss it. [*Exit Malvolio.*] Now you see, sir, how your fooling grows old, and people dislike it.

Clown. Thou hast spoke for us, madonna, as if thy eldest son should be a fool—whose skull Jove cram with brains! for here he comes,—one of thy kin has a most weak pia mater.[4]

---

[1] "The zany in Shakespeare's day was the vice, servant, or attendant of the professional clown or fool, who, dressed like his master, accompanied him on the stage or in the ring, following his movements, attempting to imitate his tricks, and adding to the general merriment by his ludicrous failures and comic imbecility." — *Edinburgh Review*, July, 1869.

[2] Short, blunt-headed arrows.

[3] Lying. The clown invokes Mercury, as this celebrated god of antiquity was the patron of thieves, cheats, and deceitful persons generally.

[4] A thin inner membrane enveloping the brain. The clown alludes to the approaching Sir Toby.

Enter SIR TOBY.

Olivia. By mine honor, half drunk. What is he at the gate, cousin?

Sir Toby. A gentleman.

Olivia. A gentleman! What gentleman?

Sir Toby. 'Tis a gentleman here — a plague o' these pickle-herring![1] How now, sot!

Clown. Good Sir Toby!

Olivia. Cousin, cousin, how have you come so early by this lethargy?

Sir Toby. Lechery! I defy lechery. There's one at the gate.

Olivia. Ay, marry, what is he?

Sir Toby. Let him be the devil, an he will, I care not: give me faith, say I. Well, it's all one. [*Exit.*

Olivia. What's a drunken man like, fool?

Clown. Like a drown'd. man, a fool and a mad man: one draught above heat makes him a fool; the second mads him;[2] and a third drowns him.

Olivia. Go thou and seek the crowner,[3] and let him sit o' my coz; for he's in the third degree of drink, he's drown'd: go, look after him.

Clown. He is but mad yet, madonna; and the fool shall look to the madman. [*Exit.*

Reënter MALVOLIO.

Malvolio. Madam, yond young fellow swears he will speak with you. I told him you were sick; he takes on him to understand so much, and therefore comes to speak with you. I told him you were asleep; he seems to have a foreknowledge of that

---

[1] Sir Toby is interrupted in his speech by a drunken hiccough, which he attributes to the pickled herring he had eaten. The clown laughing, the knight turns to him, exclaiming furiously, "How now, sot!"

[2] "One draught above heat," etc., i.e., one glass more than enough makes him a fool; the second glass maddens him, etc.

[3] Coroner.

too, and therefore comes to speak with you. What is to be said to him, lady? he's fortified against any denial.

Olivia. Tell him he shall not speak with me.

Malvolio. Has been told so; and he says he'll stand at your door like a sheriff's post,[1] and be the supporter to a bench, but he'll speak with you.

Olivia. What kind o' man is he?

Malvolio. Why, of mankind.

Olivia. What manner of man?

Malvolio. Of very ill manner; he'll speak with you, will you or no.

Olivia. Of what personage and years is he?

Malvolio. Not yet old enough for a man, nor young enough for a boy; as a squash is before 'tis a peascod, or a codling when 'tis almost an apple: 'tis with him e'en standing water, between boy and man. He is very well-favor'd and he speaks very shrewishly.

Olivia. Let him approach: call in my gentlewoman.

Malvolio. Gentlewoman, my lady calls.   [*Exit.*

Reënter MARIA.

Olivia. Give me my veil: come, throw it o'er my face.
We'll once more hear Orsino's embassy.

Enter VIOLA.

Viola. The honorable lady of the house, which is she?

Olivia. Speak to me; I shall answer for her. Your will?

Viola. Most radiant, exquisite and unmatchable beauty,— I pray you, tell me if this be the lady of the house, for I never saw her: I would be loath to cast away my speech, for besides that it is excellently well penn'd, I have taken great pains to con it.

---

[1] "Outside the sheriff's door there used to be set up painted posts, both for the purpose of showing where the sheriff lived, and for posting proclamations."

Good beauties, let me sustain no scorn; I am very comptible,[1] even to the least sinister usage.

Olivia. Whence came you, sir?

.Viola. I can say little more than I have studied, and that question's out of my part. Good gentle one, give me modest assurance if you be the lady of the house, that I may proceed in my speech.

Olivia. Are you a comedian?

Viola. No, my profound heart: and yet, by the very fangs of malice I swear, I am not that I play. Are you the lady of the house?

Olivia. If I do not usurp myself, I am.

Viola. Most certain, if you are she, you do usurp yourself; for what is yours to bestow is not yours to reserve. But this is from[2] my commission: I will on with my speech in your praise, and then show you the heart of my message.

Olivia. Come to what is important in't: I forgive you the praise.

Viola. Alas, I took great pains to study it, and 'tis poetical.

Olivia. It is the more like to be feigned: I pray you, keep it in. I heard you were saucy at my gates, and allow'd your approach rather to wonder at you than to hear you. If you be mad, be gone; if you have reason, be brief: 'tis not that time of moon with me to make one in so skipping a dialogue.

Maria. Will you hoist sail, sir? here lies your way.

Viola. No, good swabber;[3] I am to hull[3] here a little longer. Some mollification for your giant,[4] sweet lady.

---

[1] Sensitive.   [2] Out of.

[3] Viola takes up Maria's metaphor. "Swabber" is one who swabs or washes the decks of a ship; "to hull" is to float, as a vessel in a calm.

[4] "Some mollification," etc. Dr. Johnson notes that "ladies in romance are guarded by giants. Viola, seeing the waiting-maid so eager to oppose her message, entreats Olivia to pacify her 'giant.'" There is also an ironical allusion to the size of Maria, who is subsequently represented as of diminutive stature.

Olivia. Tell me your mind.

Viola. I am a messenger.

Olivia. Sure, you have some hideous matter to deliver, when the courtesy of it is so fearful. Speak your office.

Viola. It alone concerns your ear. I bring no overture of war, no taxation[1] of homage: I hold the olive[2] in my hand; my words are as full of peace as matter.

Olivia. Yet you began rudely. What are you? what would you?

Viola. The rudeness that hath appear'd in me have I learn'd from my entertainment. What I am, and what I would, are as secret as maidenhood; to your ears, divinity, to any other's, profanation.

Olivia. Give us the place alone: we will hear this divinity. [*Exit Maria.*] Now, sir, what is your text?

Viola. Most sweet lady —

Olivia. A comfortable doctrine, and much may be said of it. Where lies your text?

Viola. In Orsino's bosom.

Olivia. In his bosom! In what chapter of his bosom?

Viola. To answer by the method, in the first of his heart.

Olivia. O, I have read it: it is heresy. Have you no more to say?

Viola. Good madam, let me see your face.

Olivia. Have you any commission from your lord to negotiate with my face? You are now out of your text: but we will draw the curtain and show you the picture. Look you, sir, such a one I was this present:[3] is't not well done? [*Unveiling.*

Viola. Excellently done, if God did all.

Olivia. 'Tis in grain, sir; 'twill endure wind and weather.

Viola. 'Tis beauty truly blent, whose red and white
Nature's own sweet and cunning hand laid on:

---

[1] Exaction.   [2] An emblem of peace.

[3] " Such a one," etc., i.e., such as I am at the present moment, Olivia speaking as though she were showing Viola the picture.

Lady, you are the cruel'st she alive,
If you will lead these graces to the grave
And leave the world no copy.

.*Olivia.* O, sir, I will not be so hard-hearted; I will give out divers schedules of my beauty: it shall be inventoried, and every particle and utensil label'd to my will: as, item, two lips, indifferent[1] red; item, two gray eyes, with lids to them; item, one neck, one chin, and so forth. Were you sent hither to praise[2] me?

Viola. I see you what you are, you are too proud;
But, if you were the devil, you are fair.
My lord and master loves you: O, such love
Could be but recompens'd, though you were crown'd
The nonpareil of beauty!

Olivia. How does he love me?

Viola. With adorations, with fertile tears,
With groans that thunder love, with sighs of fire.

Olivia. Your lord does know my mind; I cannot love him:
Yet I suppose him virtuous, know him noble,
Of great estate, of fresh and stainless youth;
In voices well divulg'd, free,[3] learn'd and valiant;
And in dimension and the shape of nature
A gracious person: but yet I cannot love him;
He might have took his answer long ago.

Viola. If I did love you in my master's flame,
With such a suffering, such a deadly life,
In your denial I would find no sense;
I would not understand it.

Olivia. Why, what would you?

Viola. Make me a willow[4] cabin at your gate,
And call upon my soul within the house;

---

[1] Fairly or tolerably. [2] Appraise.
[3] "In voices well divulg'd, free," i.e., well spoken of by the world; generous.
[4] An emblem of forsaken or unhappy love.

Write loyal cantons[1] of contemned love
And sing them loud even in the dead of night;
Halloo your name to the reverberate hills
And make the babbling gossip of the air
Cry out "Olivia!"   O, you should not rest
Between the elements of air and earth,
But you should pity me!
   Olivia.   You might do much.
What is your parentage?
   Viola. Above my fortunes, yet my state is well:
I am a gentleman.
   Olivia.   Get you to your lord;
I cannot love him: let him send no more;
Unless, perchance, you come to me again,
To tell me how he takes it.   Fare you well:
I thank you for your pains: spend this for me.
   Viola. I am no fee'd post, lady; keep your purse:
My master, not myself, lacks recompense.
Love make his heart of flint that you shall love;
And let your fervor, like my master's, be
Placed in contempt!   Farewell, fair cruelty.   [*Exit.*
   Olivia. "What is your parentage?"
"Above my fortunes, yet my state is well:
I am a gentleman."   I'll be sworn thou art;
Thy tongue, thy face, thy limbs, actions and spirit,
Do give thee fivefold blason: not too fast: soft, soft!
Unless the master were the man.   How now!
Even so quickly may one catch the plague?
Methinks I feel this youth's perfections
With an invisible and subtle stealth
To creep in at mine eyes.   Well, let it be.
What ho, Malvolio!

---

[1] Cantos.

Reënter MALVOLIO.

Malvolio. Here, madam, at your service.
Olivia. Run after that same peevish messenger,
The county's man :[1] he left this ring behind him,
Would I or not: tell him I'll none of it.
Desire him not to flatter with his lord,
Nor hold him up with hopes; I am not for him:
If that the youth will come this way to-morrow,
I'll give him reasons for't: hie thee, Malvolio.
Malvolio. Madam, I will. [*Exit.*
Olivia. I do I know not what, and fear to find
Mine eye too great a flatterer for my mind.
Fate, show thy force: ourselves we do not owe ;[2]
What is decreed must be, and be this so. [*Exit.*

ACT II.

SCENE I. *The Seacoast.*

Enter ANTONIO *and* SEBASTIAN.

Antonio. Will you stay no longer? nor will you not that I go
with you?
Sebastian. By your patience, no. My stars shine darkly over
me: the malignancy of my fate might perhaps distemper yours ;[3]
therefore I shall crave of you your leave that I may bear my
evils alone: it were a bad recompense for your love, to lay any
of them on you.
Antonio. Let me yet know of you whither you are bound.

---

[1] " County's man," i.e., count's manservant. " County" for " count"
is often used in Shakespeare.

[2] Own.

[3] " My stars," etc. It was the old belief of the astrologers that a man's
destiny was influenced by the planets which were in the ascendant at his birth.
" Malignant" was an epithet commonly applied to stars.

Sebastian. No, sooth, sir: my determinate voyage is mere extravagancy.[1] But I perceive in you so excellent a touch of modesty, that you will not extort from me what I am willing[2] to keep in; therefore it charges me in manners the rather to express myself. You must know of me then, Antonio, my name is Sebastian, which I called Roderigo. My father was that Sebastian of Messaline, whom I know you have heard of. He left behind him myself and a sister, both born in an hour: if the heavens had been pleas'd, would we had so ended! but you, sir, alter'd that; for some hour before you took me from the breach of the sea was my sister drown'd.

Antonio. Alas the day!

Sebastian. A lady, sir, though it was said she much resembled me, was yet of many accounted beautiful: but, though I could not with such estimable wonder[3] overfar believe that, yet thus far I will boldly publish her; she bore a mind that envy could not but call fair. She is drown'd already, sir, with salt water, though I seem to drown her remembrance again with more.

Antonio. Pardon me, sir, your bad entertainment.

Sebastian. O good Antonio, forgive me your trouble.

Antonio. If you will not murder me for my love, let me be your servant.

Sebastian. If you will not undo what you have done, that is, kill him whom you have recover'd, desire it not. Fare ye well at once: my bosom is full of kindness, and I am yet so near the manners of my mother, that upon the least occasion more mine eyes will tell tales of me. I am bound to the Count Orsino's court: farewell.   [*Exit.*

Antonio. The gentleness[4] of all the gods go with thee!

---

[1] " My determinate," etc., i.e., my intended travel is mere roving. " Extravagancy " signifies vagrancy.

[2] Wishing.

[3] " With such estimable wonder," i.e., with the admiration which influenced such a judgment.

[4] Kindness.

I have many enemies in Orsino's court,
Else would I very shortly see thee there.
But, come what may, I do adore thee so,
That danger shall seem sport, and I will go.   [*Exit.*

Scene II.   *A Street.*

Enter VIOLA, MALVOLIO *following.*

Malvolio. Were not you ev'n now with the Countess Olivia?

Viola. Even now, sir; on a moderate pace I have since arriv'd but hither.

Malvolio. She returns this ring to you, sir: you might have saved me my pains, to have taken it away yourself. She adds, moreover, that you should put your lord into a desperate assurance she will none of him: and one thing more, that you be never so hardy to come again in his affairs, unless it be to report your lord's taking of this.   Receive it so.

Viola. She took the ring of me:[1] I'll none of it.

Malvolio. Come, sir, you peevishly threw it to her; and her will is, it should be so return'd: if it be worth stooping for, there it lies in your eye; if not, be it his that finds it.   [*Exit.*

Viola. I left no ring with her: what means this lady?
Fortune forbid my outside have not charm'd her!
She made good view of me; indeed, so much,
That sure methought her eyes had lost her tongue,
For she did speak in starts distractedly.
She loves me, sure; the cunning of her passion
Invites me in this churlish messenger.
None of my lord's ring! why, he sent her none.
I am the man: if it be so, as 'tis,
Poor lady, she were better love a dream.

---

[1] " Viola, finding the ring sent after her accompanied by a fiction, is prepared to meet it with another, and designedly avoids betraying the weakness of Olivia before her steward."

Disguise, I see, thou art a wickedness,
Wherein the pregnant enemy [1] does much.
How easy is it for the proper-false [2]
In women's waxen hearts to set their forms!
Alas, our frailty is the cause, not we!
For such as we are made of, such we be.
How will this fadge ? [3] my master loves her dearly;
And I, poor monster, [4] fond as much on him;
And she, mistaken, seems to dote on me.
What will become of this ?   As I am man,
My state is desperate for my master's love;
As I am woman,—now alas the day!—
What thriftless sighs shall poor Olivia breathe!
O time! thou must untangle this, not I;
It is too hard a knot for me to untie!   [*Exit.*

SCENE III.   *Olivia's House.*

Enter SIR TOBY *and* SIR ANDREW.

Sir Toby. Approach, Sir Andrew: not to be a-bed after
midnight is to be up betimes; and "diluculo surgere," [5] thou
know'st —

Sir Andrew. Nay, by my troth, I know not: but I know, to
be up late is to be up late.

Sir Toby. A false conclusion: I hate it as an unfill'd can.   To
be up after midnight and to go to bed then, is early: so that to
go to bed after midnight is to go to bed betimes.   Does not our
life consist of the four elements ? [6]

---

1 " Pregnant enemy," i.e., ready enemy of mankind.

2 " Proper-false," i.e., handsome and deceitful.   Double adjectives are
not infrequent in Shakespeare.

3 Suit, fit.

4 Viola refers to her disguise: a woman appearing as a man.

5 " Diluculo surgere saluberrimum est," i.e., to rise early (at dawn) is
most healthful.

6 " Four elements," i.e., earth, air, fire, and water.   These were supposed

Sir Andrew. Faith, so they say; but I think it rather consists of eating and drinking.

Sir Toby. Thou'rt a scholar; let us therefore eat and drink. Marian, I say! a stoup of wine!

Enter CLOWN.

Sir Andrew. Here comes the fool, i' faith.

Clown. How now, my hearts! did you never see the picture of "we three"? [1]

Sir Toby. Welcome, ass. Now let's have a catch.

Sir Andrew. By my troth, the fool has an excellent breast.[2] I had rather than forty shillings I had such a leg, and so sweet a breath to sing, as the fool has. In sooth, thou wast in very gracious fooling last night, when thou spokest of Pigrogromitus, of the Vapians passing the equinoctial of Queubus: [3] 'twas very good, i' faith. I sent thee sixpence for thy leman: [4] hadst it?

Clown. I did impeticos thy gratillity; [5] for Malvolio's nose is no whipstock: my lady has a white hand, and the Myrmidons are no bottle-ale houses.

Sir Andrew. Excellent! why, this is the best fooling, when all is done. Now, a song.

Sir Toby. Come on; there is sixpence for you: let's have a song.

Sir Andrew. There's a testril[6] of me too: if one knight give a —

to enter into the composition of every man, and on their proper mixture a perfect temperament and disposition depended.

[1] A picture often hung in ale-houses represented two asses with the inscription "We Three." The spectator who saw the joke rarely boasted of having seen it.

[2] Voice.   [3] See Note 1, p. 25.

[4] Sweetheart.

[5] " I did impeticos," etc. I did pocket thy gratuity, is the meaning probably, but the clown's speech was not intended to be explained: it is to be laughed at in defiance of criticism.

[6] A French coin of about sixpence value in Shakespeare's time.

Clown. Would you have a love-song, or a song of good life? [1]

Sir Toby. A love-song, a love-song.

Sir Andrew. Ay, ay: I care not for good life.

Clown. [*Sings*]

> *O mistress mine, where are you roaming?*
> *O, stay and hear; your true love's coming,*
> > *That can sing both high and low:*
> *Trip no further, pretty sweeting;*
> *Journeys end in lovers meeting,*
> > *Every wise man's son doth know.*

Sir Andrew. Excellent good, i' faith.

Sir Toby. Good, good.

Clown. [*Sings*]

> *What is love? 'tis not hereafter;*
> *Present mirth hath present laughter;*
> > *What's to come is still unsure:*
> *In delay there lies no plenty;*
> *Then come kiss me, sweet and twenty,*
> > *Youth's a stuff will not endure.*

Sir Andrew. A mellifluous voice, as I am true knight.

Sir Toby. A contagious breath.

Sir Andrew. Very sweet and contagious, i' faith.

Sir Toby. To hear by the nose, it is dulcet in contagion. But shall we make the welkin dance indeed? shall we rouse the night-owl in a catch that will draw three souls out of one weaver? [2] shall we do that?

Sir Andrew. An you love me, let's do't: I am dog at a catch.

Clown. By'r lady, sir, and some dogs will catch well.

Sir Andrew. Most certain. Let our catch be, "Thou knave."

---

[1] " A song of good life," i.e., a moral song.

[2] " To draw three souls out of one weaver can be nothing more than a humorously exaggerated consequence of the power exerted by music; and to bring this about by a drinking-song was a greater triumph still, for weavers were given to psalms."

Clown. "Hold thy peace, thou knave," knight? I shall be constrained in't to call thee knave, knight.

Sir Andrew. 'Tis not the first time I have constrained one to call me knave. Begin, fool: it begins "Hold thy peace."

Clown. I shall never begin if I hold my peace.

Sir Andrew. Good, i' faith. Come, begin. [*Catch sung.*

Enter MARIA.

Maria. What a caterwauling do you keep here! If my lady have not call'd up her steward Malvolio and bid him turn you out of doors, never trust me.

Sir Toby. My lady's a Cataian, we are politicians, Malvolio's a Peg-a-Ramsey,[1] and "Three merry men be we." Am not I consanguineous? am I not of her blood? Tillyvally.[2] Lady! [*Sings*] "*There dwelt a man in Babylon, lady, lady!*"

Clown. Beshrew me, the knight's in admirable fooling.

Sir Andrew. Ay, he does well enough if he be dispos'd, and so do I too: he does it with a better grace, but I do it more natural.

Sir Toby. [*Sings*] "*O, the twelfth day of December*"—

Maria. For the love o' God, peace!

Enter MALVOLIO.

Malvolio. My masters, are you mad? or what are you? Have you no wit, manners, nor honesty,[3] but to gabble like tinkers at this time of night? Do ye make an ale-house of my lady's house, that ye squeak out your coziers' catches without any mitigation or remorse of voice? Is there no respect of place, persons, nor time in you?

---

[1] "Cataian . . . Peg-a-Ramsey." A "Cataian" is a native of Cataia or Cathay (China). "It is supposed to have become a cant term for a thief or sharper, because the Chinese were notorious for their skillful thieving." "Peg-a-Ramsey" is the name of an old tune. Sir Toby is not in condition to choose his epithets with much judgment.

[2] An expression of contempt.   [3] Propriety.

Sir Toby. We did keep time, sir, in our catches. Sneck up![1]

Malvolio. Sir Toby, I must be round with[2] you. My lady bade me tell you, that, though she harbors you as her kinsman, she's nothing allied to your disorders. If you can separate yourself and your misdemeanors, you are welcome to the house; if not, an it would please you to take leave of her, she is very willing to bid you farewell.

Sir Toby. " Farewell, dear heart, since I must needs be gone."

Maria. Nay, good Sir Toby.

Clown. " His eyes do show his days are almost done."

Malvolio. Is't even so?

Sir Toby. " But I will never die."

Clown. Sir Toby, there you lie.

Malvolio. This is much credit to you.

Sir Toby. " Shall I bid him go? "

Clown. " What an if you do? "

Sir Toby. " Shall I bid him go, and spare not ? "

Clown. " O no, no, no, no, you dare not."

Sir Toby. Out o' time, sir: ye lie. Art any more than a steward? Dost thou think, because thou art virtuous, there shall be no more cakes and ale?[3]

Clown. Yes, by Saint Anne, and ginger shall be hot i' the mouth too.

Sir Toby. Thou'rt i' the right. Go, sir, rub your chain with crumbs.[4] A stoup of wine, Maria!

Malvolio. Mistress Mary, if you prize my lady's favor at anything more than contempt, you would not give means for this uncivil rule:[5] she shall know of it, by this hand. [*Exit.*

---

[1] " Sneck up! " i.e., go and be hanged.

[2] " Be round with," i.e., speak plainly to.

[3] " Art virtuous, there shall," etc., i.e., art so austere, no one else shall enjoy himself.

[4] Stewards wore gold and silver chains as a badge of office. Crumbs of bread were used to polish plate made of these metals.

[5] " Uncivil rule," i.e., disorderly conduct.

Maria. Go shake your ears.[1]

Sir Andrew. 'Twere as good a deed as to drink when a man's a-hungry, to challenge him the field, and then to break promise with him and make a fool of him.

Sir Toby. Do't, knight: I'll write thee a challenge; or I'll deliver thy indignation to him by word of mouth.

Maria. Sweet Sir Toby, be patient for to-night: since the youth of the count's was to-day with my lady, she is much out of quiet. For Monsieur Malvolio, let me alone with him: if I do not gull him into a nayword,[2] and make him a common recreation, do not think I have wit enough to lie straight in my bed: I know I can do it.

Sir Toby. Possess us, possess us;[3] tell us something of him.

Maria. Marry, sir, sometimes he is a kind of puritan.

Sir Andrew. O, if I thought that, I'ld beat him like a dog!

Sir Toby. What, for being a puritan? thy exquisite reason, dear knight?

Sir Andrew. I have no exquisite reason for't, but I have reason good enough.

Maria. The devil a puritan that he is, or anything constantly, but a time-pleaser;[4] an affection'd[5] ass, that cons state without book, and utters it by great swaths:[6] the best persuaded of himself, so cramm'd, as he thinks, with excellences, that it is his grounds of faith that all that look on him love him; and on that vice in him will my revenge find notable cause to work.

Sir Toby. What wilt thou do?

Maria. I will drop in his way some obscure epistles of love; wherein, by the color of his beard, the shape of his leg, the manner of his gait, the expressure of his eye, forehead, and complexion, he shall find himself most feelingly personated. I can

---

[1] Maria implies long ears; ass ears, of course.
[2] Password; byword.
[3] "Possess us," i.e., give it to us; let us know it.
[4] Time-server.   [5] Affected.
[6] Lines of grass cut and thrown together by the scythe.

write very like my lady your niece : on a forgotten matter we can hardly make distinction of our hands.

Sir Toby. Excellent! I smell a device.

Sir Andrew. I have't in my nose too.

Sir Toby. He shall think, by the letters that thou wilt drop, that they come from my niece, and that she's in love with him.

Maria. My purpose is, indeed, a horse of that color.

Sir Andrew. And your horse now would make him an ass.

Maria. Ass, I doubt not.

Sir Andrew. O, 'twill be admirable!

Maria. Sport royal, I warrant you : I know my physic will work with him. I will plant you two, and let the fool make a third, where he shall find the letter : observe his construction of it. For this night, to bed, and dream on the event. Farewell.   [*Exit.*

Sir Toby. Good night, Penthesilea.[1]

Sir Andrew. Before me, she's a good wench.

Sir Toby. She's a beagle,[2] true-bred, and one that adores me : what o' that?

Sir Andrew. I was ador'd once too.

Sir Toby. Let's to bed, knight. Thou hadst need send for more money.

Sir Andrew. If I cannot recover[3] your niece, I am a foul way out.

Sir Toby. Send for money, knight : if thou hast her not i' the end, call me cut.

Sir Andrew. If I do not, never trust me, take it how you will.

---

[1] A queen of the Amazons,— a community of women, according to an old tradition, who permitted no man to reside among them, and, fighting under the leadership of one of their own number, long constituted a formidable state. Sir Toby applies this name to Maria for the courage and spirit shown in her device to dupe the steward ; with a jocular allusion, also, to her small size as compared with that of the warrior queen.

[2] A small hunting-dog.

[3] Win.

Sir Toby. Come, come, I'll go burn some sack;[1] 'tis too late to go to bed now: come, knight; come, knight.   [*Exeunt.*

SCENE IV. *The Duke's Palace.*

Enter DUKE, VIOLA, CURIO, *and others.*

Duke. Give me some music. Now, good morrow, friends.
Now, good Cesario, but that piece of song,
That old and antique[2] song we heard last night:
Methought it did relieve my passion much,
More than light airs and recollected[3] terms
Of these most brisk and giddy-paced times:
Come, but one verse.

Curio. He is not here, so please your lordship, that should sing it.

Duke. Who was it?

Curio. Feste, the jester, my lord; a fool that the Lady Olivia's father took much delight in. He is about the house.

Duke. Seek him out, and play the tune the while.

        [*Exit Curio. Music plays.*

Come hither, boy: if ever thou shalt love,
In the sweet pangs of it remember me;
For such as I am all true lovers are,
Unstaid and skittish in all motions else,
Save in the constant image of the creature
That is belov'd. How dost thou like this tune?

Viola. It gives a very echo to the seat
Where Love is thron'd.

Duke. Thou dost speak masterly:
My life upon't, young though thou art, thine eye

---

[1] A Spanish wine. Mulled or burnt sack was a popular drink of the time.

[2] Quaint; old-fashioned.

[3] Repeated.

Hath stay'd upon some favor[1] that it loves:
Hath it not, boy?
   Viola.   A little, by your favor.
   Duke. What kind of woman is't?
   Viola.   Of your complexion.
   Duke. She is not worth thee, then. What years, i' faith?
   Viola. About your years, my lord.
   Duke. Too old, by heaven: let still the woman take
An elder than herself; so wears she to him,
So sways she level in her husband's heart:
For, boy, however we do praise ourselves,
Our fancies are more giddy and unfirm,
More longing, wavering, sooner lost and worn,
Than women's are.
   Viola.   I think it well, my lord.
   Duke. Then let thy love be younger than thyself,
Or thy affection cannot hold the bent;
For women are as roses, whose fair flower
Being once display'd, doth fall that very hour.
   Viola. And so they are: alas, that they are so;
To die, even when they to perfection grow!

Reënter CURIO *and* CLOWN.

   Duke. O, fellow, come, the song we had last night.
Mark it, Cesario, it is old and plain;
The spinsters and the knitters in the sun
And the free[2] maids that weave their thread with bones
Do use to chant it: it is silly sooth,[3]
And dallies with the innocence of love,
Like the old age.[4]

---

[1] Personal appearance. In her reply, Viola plays on the word, using it in the sense of " kindness."
[2] Free from care; happy.
[3] " Silly sooth," i.e., simple truth.
[4] " Old age," i.e., olden time.

Clown. Are you ready, sir?

Duke. Ay; prithee, sing.   [*Music.*

SONG.

Clown. *Come away, come away, death,*
And in sad cypress [1] *let me be laid;*
Fly away, fly away, breath;
I am slain by a fair cruel maid.
My shroud of white, stuck all with yew,
O, prepare it!
My part of death, no one so true
Did share it. [2]

Not a flower, not a flower sweet,
On my black coffin let there be strewn;
Not a friend, not a friend greet
My poor corpse, where my bones shall be thrown:
A thousand thousand sighs to save,
Lay me, O, where
Sad true lover never find my grave,
To weep there!

Duke. There's for thy pains.

Clown. No pains, sir; I take pleasure in singing, sir.

Duke. I'll pay thy pleasure then.

Clown. Truly, sir, and pleasure will be paid, one time or another.

Duke. Give me now leave to leave thee. [3]

Clown. Now, the melancholy god protect thee; and the tailor

---

[1] Cypress being an emblem of mourning, a coffin of cypress wood is appropriate.

[2] " My part of death," etc., i.e., "though death is a part in which every one acts his share, yet of all these actors no one is so true as I." — JOHNSON.

[3] The Duke politely requests the clown to retire. This form of dismissal is frequent in Shakespeare, though there is mock gravity in its use here by the Duke.

make thy doublet of changeable taffeta,[1] for thy mind is a very
opal.   I would have men of such constancy put to sea, that
their business might be everything and their intent everywhere;
for that's it that always makes a good voyage of nothing.
Farewell.   [*Exit.*

Duke. Let all the rest give place.
                          [*Curio and Attendants retire.*
                                Once more, Cesario,
Get thee to yond same sovereign cruelty:
Tell her, my love, more noble than the world,
Prizes not quantity of dirty lands;
The parts that fortune hath bestow'd upon her,
Tell her, I hold as giddily as fortune;
But 'tis that miracle and queen of gems
That nature pranks her in[2] attracts my soul.

Viola. But if she cannot love you, sir?

Duke. I cannot be so answer'd.

Viola.   Sooth, but you must.
Say that some lady, as perhaps there is,
Hath for your love as great a pang of heart
As you have for Olivia: you cannot love her;
You tell her so; must she not then be answer'd?

Duke. There is no woman's sides
Can bide the beating of so strong a passion
As love doth give my heart; no woman's heart
So big, to hold so much; they lack retention.
Alas, their love may be call'd appetite,
No motion of the liver, but the palate,
That suffers surfeit, cloyment and revolt;
But mine is all as hungry as the sea
And can digest as much: make no compare

---

[1] " Changeable taffeta," i.e., a taffeta or silk stuff in which the colors are
so woven that they vary to appearance according to the light in which the
silk is seen, in this respect resembling opal.

[2] " Pranks her in," i.e., adorns her with.

Between that love a woman can bear me
And that I owe Olivia.
 Viola.   Ay, but I know—
 .Duke. What dost thou know?
 Viola. Too well what love women to men may owe:
In faith, they are as true of heart as we.
My father had a daughter lov'd a man,
As it might be, perhaps, were I a woman,
I should your lordship.
 Duke.   And what's her history?
 Viola. A blank, my lord. She never told her love,
But let concealment, like a worm i' the bud,
Feed on her damask-cheek: she pin'd in thought,
And with a green and yellow melancholy
She sat, like Patience on a monument,
Smiling at grief. Was not this love indeed?
We men may say more, swear more: but indeed
Our shows are more than will; for still we prove
Much in our vows, but little in our love.
 Duke. But died thy sister of her love, my boy?
 Viola. I am all the daughters of my father's house,
And all the brothers too: and yet I know not.
Sir, shall I to this lady?
 Duke.   Ay, that's the theme.
To her in haste; give her this jewel; say,
My love can give no place, bide no denay.[1]   [*Exeunt.*

Scene V. *Olivia's Garden.*

Enter Sir Toby, Sir Andrew, *and* Fabian.

 Sir Toby. Come thy ways, Signior Fabian.
 Fabian. Nay, I'll come: if I lose a scruple of this sport, let
me be boil'd to death with melancholy.

---

[1] Denial.

Sir Toby. Wouldst thou not be glad to have the niggardly rascally sheep-biter[1] come by some notable shame?

Fabian. I would exult, man: you know, he brought me out o' favor with my lady about a bear-baiting here.

Sir Toby. To anger him we'll have the bear again; and we will fool him black and blue: shall we not, Sir Andrew?

Sir Andrew. An we do not, it is pity of our lives.

Sir Toby. Here comes the little villain.

Enter MARIA.

How now, my metal of India![2]

Maria. Get ye all three into the box-tree: Malvolio's coming down this walk: he has been yonder i' the sun practicing behavior to his own shadow this half-hour: observe him, for the love of mockery; for I know this letter will make a contemplative idiot of him. Close, in the name of jesting! Lie thou there [*throws down a letter*]; for here comes the trout that must be caught with tickling. [*Exit.*

Enter MALVOLIO.

Malvolio. 'Tis but fortune; all is fortune. Maria once told me she did affect me: and I have heard herself come thus near, that, should she fancy, it should be one of my complexion.[3] Besides, she uses me with a more exalted respect than any one else that follows her. What should I think on't?

Sir Toby. Here's an overweening rogue!

Fabian. O, peace! Contemplation makes a rare turkey-cock of him: how he jets under his advanc'd plumes![4]

Sir Andrew. 'Slight, I could so beat the rogue!

Sir Toby. Peace, I say.

---

[1] A morose, censorious fellow.

[2] " Metal of India," i.e., precious girl.

[3] Disposition, temperament, as indicated by outward appearance.

[4] " Jets under his," etc., i.e., struts with raised feathers, like a turkey-cock when excited.

4

Malvolio. To be Count Malvolio!

Sir Toby. Ah, rogue!

Sir Andrew. Pistol him, pistol him.

Sir Toby. Peace, peace!

Malvolio. There is example for't; the lady of the Strachy married the yeoman of the wardrobe.

Sir Andrew. Fie on him, Jezebel!

Fabian. O, peace! now he's deeply in: look how imagination blows him.   *✔*

Malvolio. Having been three months married to her, sitting in my state—

Sir Toby. O, for a stone-bow,[1] to hit him in the eye!

Malvolio. Calling my officers about me, in my branch'd velvet gown, and after a demure travel of regard,[2] telling them I know my place as I would they should do theirs, to ask for my kinsman Toby—

Sir Toby. Bolts and shackles!

Fabian. O peace, peace, peace! now, now.

Malvolio. Seven of my people, with an obedient start, make out for him: I frown the while; and perchance wind up my watch,[3] or play with my—some rich jewel.[4] Toby approaches; courtesies there to me—

Sir Toby. Shall this fellow live?

Fabian. Though our silence be drawn from us with cords, yet peace.

Malvolio. I extend my hand to him thus, quenching my familiar smile with an austere regard of control [5]—

Sir Toby. And does not Toby take you a blow o' the lips then?

---

[1] A bow for throwing stones.

[2] "After a demure," etc., i.e., after slowly and gravely staring around.

[3] The first watches used in England were introduced from Germany about the year 1580, when Shakespeare was a lad of sixteen.

[4] Malvolio is about to say " chain," but, remembering his altered fortunes, substitutes something more appropriate than the steward's badge.

[5] "Austere regard," etc., i.e., stern, authoritative look.

Malvolio. Saying, "Cousin Toby, my fortunes having cast me on your niece give me this prerogative of speech"—

Sir Toby. What, what?

Malvolio. "You must amend your drunkenness."

Sir Toby. Out, patch!

Fabian. Nay, patience, or we break the sinews of our plot.

Malvolio. "Besides, you waste the treasure of your time with a foolish knight"—

Sir Andrew. That's me, I warrant you.

Malvolio. "One Sir Andrew"—

Sir Andrew. I knew 'twas I; for many do call me fool.

Malvolio. What employment have we here?

[*Taking up the letter.*

Fabian. Now is the woodcock near the gin.

Sir Toby. O, peace! and the spirit of humors intimate reading aloud to him!

Malvolio. By my life, this is my lady's hand: these be her very *C*'s, her *U*'s and her *T*'s; and thus makes she her great *P*'s. It is, in contempt of question, her hand.

Sir Andrew. Her *C*'s, her *U*'s and her *T*'s: why that?

Malvolio. [*Reads*] "*To the unknown beloved, this, and my good wishes:*"—her very phrases! By your leave, wax. Soft! and the impressure her Lucrece, with which she uses to seal; 'tis my lady. To whom should this be?

Fabian. This wins him, liver and all.

Malvolio. [*Reads*] "*Jove knows I love:*
            But who?
         Lips, do not move;
         No man must know."

"No man must know." What follows? the numbers alter'd![1]
"No man must know:" if this should be thee, Malvolio?

Sir Toby. Marry, hang thee, brock![2]

---

[1] "The numbers alter'd," i.e., the measure changed, as we see when Malvolio reads again.

[2] Badger; often used as a term of contempt.

Malvolio. [*Reads*]

"*I may command where I adore;*
But silence, like a Lucrece knife,
With bloodless stroke my heart doth gore:
M, O, A, I, doth sway my life."

Fabian. A fustian riddle!

Sir Toby. Excellent wench, say I.

Malvolio. "*M, O, A, I,* doth sway my life." Nay, but first, let me see, let me see, let me see.

Fabian. What dish o' poison has she dress'd him!

Sir Toby. And with what wing the staniel checks at it![1]

Malvolio. "I may command where I adore." Why, she may command me: I serve her; she is my lady. Why, this is evident to any formal[2] capacity; there is no obstruction in this: and the end—what should that alphabetical position portend? If I could make that resemble something in me—Softly! *M, O, A, I*—

Sir Toby. O, ay, make up that: he is now at a cold scent.

Fabian. Sowter[3] will cry upon't for all this, though it be as rank as a fox.

Malvolio. *M*—Malvolio; *M*—why, that begins my name.

Fabian. Did not I say he would work it out? the cur is excellent at faults.[4]

Malvolio. *M*—but then there is no consonancy in the sequel; that suffers under probation;[5] *A* should follow, but *O* does.

Fabian. And *O* shall end, I hope.

Sir Toby. Ay, or I'll cudgel him, and make him cry O!

Malvolio. And then *I* comes behind.

Fabian. Ay, an you had any eye behind you, you might see more detraction at your heels than fortunes before you.

---

[1] The staniel is a kind of hawk. "Checks" is a technical term in falconry, signifying the diversion of the falcon from his proper quarry by the sight of some other prey, upon which he pounces instead.

[2] Reasonable or reasoning.

[3] A name for a hound; here applied contemptuously to Malvolio.

[4] The loss or confusion of the trail by hunting-dogs.   [5] Examination.

Malvolio. M, O, A, I; this simulation is not as the former : and yet, to crush this a little, it would bow to me, for every one of these letters are in my name. Soft! here follows prose.

[*Reads*] "*If this fall into thy hand, revolve. In my stars I am above thee; but be not afraid of greatness : some are born great, some achieve greatness and some have greatness thrust upon 'em. Thy Fates open their hands; let thy blood and spirit embrace them; and, to inure thyself to what thou art like to be, cast thy humble slough and appear fresh. Be opposite with a kinsman, surly with servants; let thy tongue tang* [1] *arguments of state; put thyself into the trick of singularity:* [2] *she thus advises thee that sighs for thee. Remember who commended thy yellow stockings, and wish'd to see thee ever cross-garter'd: I say, remember. Go to, thou art made, if thou desirest to be so; if not, let me see thee a steward still, the fellow of servants, and not worthy to touch Fortune's fingers. Farewell. She that would alter services with thee,*

"THE FORTUNATE-UNHAPPY."

Daylight and champain [3] discovers not more : this is open. I will be proud, I will read politic authors, I will baffle Sir Toby, I will wash off gross acquaintance, I will be point-devise [4] the very man. I do not now fool myself, to let imagination jade me ; for every reason excites to this, that my lady loves me. She did commend my yellow stockings of late, she did praise my leg being cross-garter'd ; and in this she manifests herself to my love, and with a kind of injunction drives me to these habits of her liking. I thank my stars I am happy. I will be strange, [5] stout, [6] in yellow stockings, and cross-garter'd, even with the swiftness of putting on. Jove and my stars be praised! Here is yet a postscript.

[*Reads*] " *Thou canst not choose but know who I am. If thou entertainest my love, let it appear in thy smiling; thy smiles become thee well; therefore in my presence still smile, dear my sweet, I prithee.*"

Jove, I thank thee : I will smile ; I will do everything that thou wilt have me. [*Exit.*

[1] Twang; clatter.   [2] Being eccentric.   [3] Champaign.
[4] Exactly.   [5] Disdainfully reserved.   [6] Proud; overbearing.

Fabian. I will not give my part of this sport for a pension of thousands to be paid from the Sophy.[1]

Sir Toby. I could marry this wench for this device.

Sir Andrew. So could I too.

Sir Toby. And ask no other dowry with her but such another jest.

Sir Andrew. Nor I neither.

Fabian. Here comes my noble gull-catcher.

Reënter MARIA.

Sir Toby. Wilt thou set thy foot o' my neck?

Sir Andrew. Or o' mine either?

Sir Toby. Shall I play my freedom at tray-trip,[2] and become thy bond-slave?

Sir Andrew. I' faith, or I either?

Sir Toby. Why, thou hast put him in such a dream, that when the image of it leaves him he must run mad.

Maria. Nay, but say true; does it work upon him?

Sir Toby. Like aqua-vitæ.[3]

Maria. If you will then see the fruits of the sport, mark his first approach before my lady: he will come to her in yellow stockings, and 'tis a color she abhors, and cross-garter'd, a fashion she detests; and he will smile upon her, which will now be so unsuitable to her disposition, being addicted to a melancholy as she is, that it cannot but turn him into a notable contempt. If you will see it, follow me.

Sir Toby. To the gates of Tartar,[4] thou most excellent devil of wit!

Sir Andrew. I'll make one too. [*Exeunt.*

---

[1] The Shah of Persia.

[2] A game played with dice.

[3] Water of life; strong spirits; brandy.

[4] Tartarus; hell.

ACT III.

Scene I. *Olivia's Garden.*

Enter VIOLA, *and* CLOWN *with a tabor.*

Viola. Save thee, friend, and thy music: dost thou live by thy tabor?

Clown. No, sir, I live by the church.

Viola. Art thou a churchman?

Clown. No such matter, sir: I do live by the church; for I do live at my house, and my house doth stand by the church.

Viola. So thou mayst say, the king lies by a beggar, if a beggar dwell near him; or, the church stands by thy tabor, if thy tabor stand by the church.

Clown. You have said, sir. To see this age! A sentence is but a cheveril[1] glove to a good wit: how quickly the wrong side may be turn'd outward!

Viola. Nay, that's certain; they that dally nicely with words may quickly make them wanton.

Clown. But indeed words are very rascals since bonds disgrac'd them.

Viola. Thy reason, man?

Clown. Troth, sir, I can yield you none without words; and words are grown so false, I am loath to prove reason with them.

Viola. I warrant thou art a merry fellow and car'st for nothing.

Clown. Not so, sir, I do care for something; but in my conscience, sir, I do not care for you: if that be to care for nothing, sir, I would it would make you invisible.

Viola. Art not thou the Lady Olivia's fool?

Clown. No, indeed, sir; the Lady Olivia has no folly: she will keep no fool, sir, till she be married; and fools are as like husbands as pilchards[2] are to herrings; the husband's the bigger: I am indeed not her fool, but her corrupter of words.

[1] Kid.　　　　[2] Fish much like herring.

Viola. I saw thee late at the Count Orsino's.

Clown. Foolery, sir, does walk about the orb like the sun, it shines everywhere. I would be sorry, sir, but the fool should be as oft with your master as with my mistress : I think I saw your wisdom there.

Viola. Nay, and thou pass[1] upon me, I'll no more with thee. Hold, there's expenses for thee.　　　　　　　*[Gives money.*

Clown. Now Jove, in his next commodity[2] of hair, send thee a beard!

Viola. By my troth, I'll tell thee, I am almost sick for one ; [*Aside*] though I would not have it grow on my chin. Is thy lady within ?

Clown. Would not a pair of these have bred, sir ?

Viola. Yes, being kept together and put to use.[3]

Clown. I would play Lord Pandarus of Phrygia, sir, to bring a Cressida to this Troilus.

Viola. I understand you, sir; 'tis well begg'd. *[Gives again.*

Clown. The matter, I hope, is not great, sir, begging but a beggar : Cressida was a beggar. My lady is within, sir. I will construe to them whence you come ; who you are and what you would are out of my welkin, I might say " element," but the word is over-worn.　　　　　　　　　　　　*[Exit.*

Viola. This fellow is wise enough to play the fool;
And to do that well craves a kind of wit :
He must observe their mood on whom he jests,
The quality of persons, and the time,
Not, like the haggard,[4] check at every feather[5]
That comes before his eye. This is a practice
As full of labor as a wise man's art :
For folly that he wisely shows is fit ;
But wise men's folly shown, quite taints their wit.

---

[1] Play your wit.　　　[2] Shipment or cargo.　　　[3] Usury ; interest.
[4] An untrained hawk or falcon.　　　[5] See Note 1, p. 52.

Enter Sir Toby *and* Sir Andrew.

Sir Toby. Save you, gentleman.

Viola. And you, sir.

Sir Andrew. Dieu vous garde, monsieur.[1]

Viola. Et vous aussi; votre serviteur.[1]

Sir Andrew. I hope, sir, you are; and I am yours.

Sir Toby. Will you encounter the house? my niece is desirous you should enter, if your trade be to her.

Viola. I am bound to your niece, sir; I mean, she is the list[2] of my voyage.

Sir Toby. Taste your legs, sir; put them to motion.

Viola. My legs do better understand me, sir, than I understand what you mean by bidding me taste my legs.

Sir Toby. I mean, to go, sir, to enter.

Viola. I will answer you with gait and entrance. But we are prevented.[3]

Enter Olivia *and* Maria.

Most excellent accomplish'd lady, the heavens rain odors on you!

Sir Andrew. That youth's a rare courtier: "Rain odors;" well.

Viola. My matter hath no voice, lady, but to your own most pregnant and vouchsafed ear.

Sir Andrew. "Odors," "pregnant" and "vouchsafed:" I'll get 'em all three all ready.

Olivia. Let the garden door be shut, and leave me to my hearing. [*Exeunt Sir Toby, Sir Andrew, and Maria.*] Give me your hand, sir.

Viola. My duty, madam, and most humble service.

---

[1] "Dieu vous garde," etc., i.e., "God protect you, sir." "Et vous aussi," etc., i.e., "And you also; your servant." Shakespeare here satirizes a prevalent affectation of introducing French phrases into conversation. Sir Andrew had caught some familiar expressions, and is airing one of them for Viola's benefit. Viola humors his conceit, and replies in the same strain.

[2] Limit.   [3] Anticipated.

Olivia. What is your name?

Viola. Cesario is your servant's name, fair princess.

Olivia. My servant, sir! 'Twas never merry world
Since lowly feigning was call'd compliment:
You're servant to the Count Orsino, youth.

Viola. And he is yours, and his must needs be yours:
Your servant's servant is your servant, madam.

Olivia. For him, I think not on him: for his thoughts,
Would they were blanks, rather than fill'd with me!

Viola. Madam, I come to whet your gentle thoughts
On his behalf.

Olivia.   O, by your leave, I pray you,
I bade you never speak again of him:
But, would you undertake another suit,
I had rather hear you to solicit that
Than music from the spheres.[1]

Viola.   Dear lady —

Olivia. Give me leave, beseech you. I did send,
After the last enchantment you did here,
A ring in chase of you: so did I abuse
Myself, my servant and, I fear me, you:
Under your hard construction must I sit,
To force that on you, in a shameful cunning,
Which you knew none of yours: what might you think?
Have you not set mine honor at the stake
And baited it with all the unmuzzled thoughts
That tyrannous heart can think? To one of your receiving[2]
Enough is shown: a cypress,[3] not a bosom,
Hideth my heart. So, let me hear you speak.

Viola. I pity you.

Olivia.   That's a degree to love.

---

[1] It was the doctrine of Pythagoras that the stars in their revolution produced a heavenly music.

[2] Ready apprehension.

[3] A thin, semi-transparent fabric.

Viola. No, not a grise;[1] for 'tis a vulgar proof,[2]
That very oft we pity enemies.
Olivia. Why, then, methinks 'tis time to smile again.
O world, how apt the poor are to be proud!
If one should be a prey, how much the better
To fall before the lion than the wolf!   [*Clock strikes.*
The clock upbraids me with the waste of time.
Be not afraid, good youth, I will not have you:
And yet, when wit and youth is come to harvest,
Your wife is like to reap a proper man:
There lies your way, due west.
Viola. Then westward-ho![3] Grace and good disposition
Attend your ladyship!
You'll nothing, madam, to my lord by me?
Olivia. Stay:
I prithee, tell me what thou think'st of me.
Viola. That you do think you are not what you are.
Olivia. If I think so, I think the same of you.
Viola. Then think you right: I am not what I am.
Olivia. I would you were as I would have you be!
Viola. Would it be better, madam, than I am?
I wish it might, for now I am your fool.
Olivia. O, what a deal of scorn looks beautiful
In the contempt and anger of his lip!
A murd'rous guilt shows not itself more soon
Than love that would seem hid: love's night is noon.
Cesario, by the roses of the spring,
By maidhood, honor, truth and everything,
I love thee so, that, mauger[4] all thy pride,
Nor wit nor reason can my passion hide.

---

1 Step.

2 "Vulgar proof," i.e., a thing of every-day experience.

3 "Westward-ho!" and "Eastward-ho!" were cries of the boatmen on
the Thames.

4 In spite of.

Do not extort thy reasons from this clause,
For that[1] I woo, thou therefore hast no cause;
But rather reason thus with reason fetter,
Love sought is good, but given unsought is better.

Viola. By innocence I swear, and by my youth,
I have one heart, one bosom and one truth,
And that no woman has; nor never none
Shall mistress be of it, save I alone.
And so adieu, good madam: never more
Will I my master's tears to you deplore.

Olivia. Yet come again; for thou perhaps mayst move
That heart, which now abhors, to like his love.   [*Exeunt.*

Scene II. *Olivia's House.*

Enter Sir Toby, Sir Andrew, *and* Fabian.

Sir Andrew. No, faith, I'll not stay a jot longer.

Sir Toby. Thy reason, dear venom, give thy reason.

Fabian. You must needs yield your reason, Sir Andrew.

Sir Andrew. Marry, I saw your niece do more favors to the count's serving-man than ever she bestow'd upon me; I saw't i' the orchard.

Sir Toby. Did she see thee the while, old boy? tell me that.

Sir Andrew. As plain as I see you now.

Fabian. This was a great argument of love in her toward you.

Sir Andrew. 'Slight, will you make an ass o' me?

Fabian. I will prove it legitimate, sir, upon the oaths of judgment and reason.

Sir Toby. And they have been grand-jurymen since before Noah was a sailor.

Fabian. She did show favor to the youth in your sight only to exaspcrate you, to awaken your dormouse valor, to put fire in your heart, and brimstone in your liver. You should then have

---

1 " For that," i.e., because.

accosted her; and with some excellent jests, fire-new from the mint, you should have bang'd the youth into dumbness. This was look'd for at your hand, and this was balk'd: the double guilt of this opportunity you let time wash off, and you are now sail'd into the north of my lady's opinion; where you will hang like an icicle on a Dutchman's beard, unless you do redeem it by some laudable attempt either of valor or policy.

Sir Andrew. An't be any way, it must be with valor; for policy I hate: I had as lief be a Brownist[1] as a politician.[2]

Sir Toby. Why, then, build me thy fortunes upon the basis of valor. Challenge me[3] the count's youth to fight with him; hurt him in eleven places: my niece shall take note of it; and assure thyself, there is no love-broker in the world can more prevail in man's commendation with woman than report of valor.

Fabian. There is no way but this, Sir Andrew.

Sir Andrew. Will either of you bear me a challenge to him?

Sir Toby. Go, write it in a martial hand; be curst[4] and brief; it is no matter how witty, so it be eloquent and full of invention: taunt him with the license of ink: if thou thou'st[5] him some thrice, it shall not be amiss; and as many lies as will lie in thy sheet of paper, although the sheet were big enough for the bed of Ware[6] in England, set 'em down: go, about it. Let there be gall enough in thy ink; though thou write with a goose-pen, no matter: about it.

Sir Andrew. Where shall I find you?

---

[1] The Brownists were a sect of Puritans, so named from their founder, Robert Brown, who separated himself from the Church of England about the year 1580.

[2] "This word is generally used by Shakespeare in an unfavorable sense, as denoting a political intriguer."

[3] This redundant "me" was often used colloquially, and occurs frequently in Shakespeare's plays.

[4] Surly.

[5] To use "thou" in addressing strangers who were not inferiors was highly offensive.

[6] This celebrated bed is carefully preserved as a Shakespearian relic. It

Sir Toby. We'll call thee at the cubiculo :[1] go.

[*Exit Sir Andrew.*

Fabian. This is a dear manikin[2] to you, Sir Toby.

Sir·Toby. I have been dear to him, lad, some two thousand strong, or so.

Fabian. We shall have a rare letter from him : but you'll not deliver't?

Sir Toby. Never trust me, then ; and by all means stir on the youth to an answer. I think oxen and wainropes cannot hale them together. For Andrew, if he were open'd, and you find so much blood in his liver as will clog the foot of a flea, I'll eat the rest of the anatomy.

Fabian. And his opposite,[3] the youth, bears in his visage no great presage of cruelty.

Enter MARIA.

Sir Toby. Look, where the youngest wren of nine[4] comes.

Maria. If you desire the spleen,[5] and will laugh yourselves into stitches, follow me. Yond gull Malvolio is turn'd heathen, a very renegado ; for there is no Christian, that means to be saved by believing rightly, can ever believe such impossible passages of grossness. He's in yellow stockings.

Sir Toby. And cross-garter'd?

Maria. Most villainously ; like a pedant that keeps a school i' the church. I have dogg'd him, like his murderer. He does obey every point of the letter that I dropp'd to betray him : he

was sold at auction in 1869, bringing five hundred dollars. The old piece of furniture is of oak, richly carved, over seven feet in height, and about eleven feet square.

1 Lodgings.

2 Little man : used contemptuously. 3 Adversary.

4 Another reference to Maria's diminutive size. The wren usually lays eight to ten eggs, and of the young birds the last hatched is said to be the smallest.

5 Immoderate laughter was supposed to have the effect of enlarging the spleen.

does smile his face into more lines than is in the new map with
the augmentation of the Indies :[1] you have not seen such a thing
as 'tis.   I can hardly forbear hurling things at him.   I know my
lady will strike him: if she do, he'll smile and take't for a great
favor.

Sir Toby.   Come, bring us, bring us where he is.   [*Exeunt.*

Scene III.   *A Street.*

Enter SEBASTIAN *and* ANTONIO.

Sebastian.   I would not by my will have troubled you ;
But, since you make your pleasure of your pains,
I will no further chide you.

Antonio.   I could not stay behind you: my desire,
More sharp than filed steel, did spur me forth ;
And not all love to see you, though so much
As might have drawn one to a longer voyage,
But jealousy[2] what might befall your travel,
Being skill-less in these parts ; which to a stranger,
Unguided and unfriended, often prove
Rough and unhospitable : my willing love,
The rather by these arguments of fear,
Set forth in your pursuit.   ·

Sebastian.   My kind Antonio,
I can no other answer make but thanks,
And thanks, and thanks ; and ever oft good turns
Are shuffled off with such uncurrent pay !
But, were my worth[3] as is my conscience firm,
You should find better dealing.   What's to do?
Shall we go see the reliques of this town?

---

[1] This refers to a map published in an edition of Hakluyt's Voyages
(1599–1600), in which the East Indies are given in greater detail than in any
previous map.

[2] Apprehension.   [3] Wealth.

Antonio. To-morrow, sir: best first go see your lodging.

Sebastian. I am not weary, and 'tis long to night:
I pray you, let us satisfy our eyes
With the memorials and the things of fame
That do renown this city.

Antonio. Would you'ld pardon me;
I do not without danger walk these streets:
Once, in a sea-fight, 'gainst the count his[1] galleys
I did some service; of such note indeed,
That were I ta'en here it would[2] scarce be answer'd.

Sebastian. Belike you slew great number of his people.

Antonio. The offense is not of such a bloody nature;
Albeit the quality of the time and quarrel
Might well have given us bloody argument.
It might have since been answer'd in repaying
What we took from them; which, for traffic sake,
Most of our city did: only myself stood out;
For which, if I be lapsed[3] in this place,
I shall pay dear.

Sebastian. Do not then walk too open.

Antonio. It doth not fit me. Hold, sir, here's my purse.
In the south suburbs, at the Elephant,
Is best to lodge: I will bespeak our diet,
Whiles you beguile the time and feed your knowledge
With viewing of the town: there shall you have me.[4]

Sebastian. Why I your purse?

Antonio. Haply your eye shall light upon some toy
You have desire to purchase; and your store,
I think, is not for idle markets, sir.

Sebastian. I'll be your purse-bearer and leave you
For an hour.

1 " Count his galleys," i.e., galleys belonging to the count.
2 Could.
3 Here used in the sense of " surprised," " caught."
4 Find me.

Antonio. To the Elephant.

Sebastian. I do remember. [*Exeunt.*

SCENE IV. *Olivia's Garden.*

Enter OLIVIA *and* MARIA.

Olivia. I have sent after him : he says he'll come ;[1]
How shall I feast him? what bestow of[2] him?
For youth is bought more oft than begg'd or borrow'd.
I speak too loud.
Where is Malvolio? he is sad and civil,
And suits well for a servant with my fortunes :
Where is Malvolio?

Maria. He's coming, madam ; but in very strange manner.
He is, sure, possess'd, madam.

Olivia. Why, what's the matter? does he rave?

Maria. No, madam, he does nothing but smile : your ladyship
were best to have some guard about you, if he comes ; for, sure,
the man is tainted in's wits.

Olivia. Go call him hither. [*Exit Maria.*] I am as mad as he,
If sad and merry madness equal be.

Reënter MARIA, *with* MALVOLIO.

How now, Malvolio ?

Malvolio. Sweet lady, ho, ho.

Olivia. Smil'st thou?
I sent for thee upon a sad occasion.

Malvolio. Sad, lady! I could be sad : this does make some
obstruction in the blood, this cross-gartering ; but what of that?
if it please the eye of one, it is with me as the very true sonnet
is, " Please one, and please all."

---

[1] This is to be understood hypothetically, " Suppose he says he'll
come? " Olivia's messenger had not yet returned.
[2] On.

Olivia. Why, how dost thou, man? what is the matter with thee?

Malvolio. Not black in my mind, though yellow in my legs. It did come to his hands, and commands shall be executed: I think we do know the sweet Roman hand.

Olivia. Wilt thou go to bed, Malvolio?

Malvolio. To bed! ay, sweet-heart, if it'll please thee.

Olivia. God comfort thee! Why dost thou smile so and kiss thy hand so oft!

Maria. How do you, Malvolio?

Malvolio. At your request! yes; nightingales answer daws.

Maria. Why appear you with this ridiculous boldness before my lady?

Malvolio. " Be not afraid of greatness:" 'twas well writ.

Olivia. What mean'st thou by that, Malvolio?

Malvolio. " Some are born great " —

Olivia. Ha!

Malvolio. " Some achieve greatness " —

Olivia. What say'st thou?

Malvolio. " And some have greatness thrust upon them."

Olivia. Heaven restore thee!

Malvolio. " Remember who commended thy yellow stockings " —

Olivia. Thy yellow stockings!

Malvolio. " And wish'd to see thee cross-garter'd."

Olivia. Cross-garter'd!

Malvolio. " Go to, thou art made, if thou desir'st to be so " —

Olivia. Am I made?

Malvolio. " If not, let me see thee a servant still."

Olivia. Why, this is very midsummer madness.

Enter Servant.

Servant. Madam, the young gentleman of the Count Orsino's is return'd: I could hardly entreat him back: he attends your ladyship's pleasure.

Olivia. I'll come to him. [*Exit Servant.*] Good Maria, let this fellow be look'd to. Where's my cousin Toby? Let some of my people have a special care of him: I would not have him miscarry for the half of my dowry. [*Exeunt Olivia and Maria.*

Malvolio. O, ho! do you come near me now? no worse man than Sir Toby to look to me! This concurs directly with the letter: she sends him on purpose, that I may appear stubborn to him; for she incites me to that in the letter. " Cast thy humble slough," says she; "be opposite with a kinsman, surly with servants; let thy tongue tang with arguments of state; put thyself into the trick of singularity;" and consequently sets down the manner how; as, a sad face, a reverend carriage, a slow tongue, in the habit of some sir of note, and so forth. I have lim'd[1] her; but it is Jove's doing, and Jove make me thankful! And when she went away now, " Let this fellow be look'd to:" fellow! not Malvolio, nor after my degree, but fellow.[2] Why, everything adheres together, that no dram of a scruple, no scruple of a scruple, no obstacle, no incredulous[3] or unsafe circumstance — What can be said? Nothing that can be can come between me and the full prospect of my hopes. Well, Jove, not I, is the doer of this, and he is to be thanked.

Reënter MARIA, *with* SIR TOBY *and* FABIAN.

Sir Toby. Which way is he, in the name of sanctity? If all the devils of hell be drawn in little, and Legion[4] himself possess'd him, yet I'll speak to him.

Fabian. Here he is, here he is. How is't with you, sir? how is't with you, man?

Malvolio. Go off; I discard you: let me enjoy my private: go off.

---

[1] Caught, as with bird-lime.

[2] Malvolio construes the word as having been used by Olivia in the sense of " companionship," " equality."

[3] Incredible.

[4] See Mark v. 9.

Maria. Lo, how hollow the fiend speaks within him! did not I tell you? Sir Toby, my lady prays you to have a care of him.

Malvolio. Ah, ha! does she so?

Sir Toby. Go to, go to; peace, peace; we must deal gently with him: let me alone. How do you, Malvolio? how is't with you? What, man! defy the devil: consider, he's an enemy to mankind.

Malvolio. Do you know what you say?

Maria. La you, an you speak ill of the devil, how he takes it at heart! Pray God, he be not bewitch'd! My lady would not lose him for more than I'll say.

Malvolio. How now, mistress!

Maria. O Lord!

Sir Toby. Prithee, hold thy peace; this is not the way: do you not see you move him? let me alone with him.

Fabian. No way but gentleness; gently, gently: the fiend is rough, and will not be roughly us'd.

Sir Toby. Why, how now, my bawcock![1] how dost thou, chuck?

Malvolio. Sir!

Sir Toby. Ay, Biddy, come with me.[2] What, man! 'tis not for gravity to play at cherry-pit[3] with Satan: hang him, foul collier!

Maria. Get him to say his prayers, good Sir Toby, get him to pray.

Malvolio. My prayers, minx!

Maria. No, I warrant you, he will not hear of godliness.

Malvolio. Go, hang yourselves all! you are idle shallow things: I am not of your element: you shall know more hereafter. [*Exit.*

Sir Toby. Is't possible?

---

[1] Fine fellow, a term of encouragement.

[2] " Ay, Biddy, come with me," are in all probability words from an old song.

[3] A game played by pitching cherry-stones into a small hole.

Fabian. If this were play'd upon a stage now, I could condemn it as an improbable fiction.

Sir Toby. His very genius hath taken the infection of[1] the device, man.

Maria. Nay, pursue him now, lest the device take air and taint.

Fabian. Why, we shall make him mad indeed.

Maria. The house will be the quieter.

Sir Toby. Come, we'll have him in a dark room and bound. My niece is already in the belief that he's mad : we may carry it thus, for our pleasure and his penance, till our very pastime, tired out of breath, prompt us to have mercy on him : at which time we will bring the device to the bar and crown thee for a finder of madmen. But see, but see.

Enter SIR ANDREW.

Fabian. More matter for a May morning.[2]

Sir Andrew. Here's the challenge, read it : I warrant there's vinegar and pepper in't.

Fabian. Is't so saucy?

Sir Andrew. Ay, is't, I warrant him : do but read.

Sir Toby. Give me. [*Reads*] *" Youth, whatsoever thou art, thou art but a scurvy fellow."*

Fabian. Good, and valiant.

Sir Toby. [*Reads*] *"Wonder not, nor admire not in thy mind, why I do call thee so, for I will show thee no reason for't."*

Fabian. A good note ; that keeps you from the blow of the law.

Sir Toby. [*Reads*] *" Thou comest to the Lady Olivia, and in my sight she uses thee kindly: but thou liest in thy throat; that is not the matter I challenge thee for."*

Fabian. Very brief, and to exceeding good sense — less.

---

1 " His very genius," etc., i.e., his whole nature is infected with.

2 Alluding to May-day sports, the 1st of May being given up to merriment and amusements of all kinds.

Sir Toby. [*Reads*] "*I will waylay thee going home; where if it be thy chance to kill me*" —

Fabian. Good.

Sir Toby. [*Reads*] "*Thou killest me like a rogue and a villain.*"

Fabian. Still you keep o' the windy side of the law: good.

Sir Toby. [*Reads*] "*Fare thee well; and God have mercy upon one of our souls! He may have mercy upon mine; but my hope is better, and so look to thyself. Thy friend, as thou usest him, and thy sworn enemy,*

" ANDREW AGUECHEEK."

If this letter move him not, his legs cannot: I'll give't him.

Maria. You may have very fit occasion for't: he is now in some commerce with my lady, and will by and by depart.

Sir Toby. Go, Sir Andrew; scout me for him at the corner of the orchard like a bum-baily;[1] so soon as ever thou seest him, draw; and, as thou draw'st, swear horrible; for it comes to pass oft that a terrible oath, with a swaggering accent sharply twang'd off, gives manhood more approbation than ever proof itself would have earn'd him. Away!

Sir Andrew. Nay, let me alone for swearing.   [*Exit.*

Sir Toby. Now will not I deliver his letter: for the behavior of the young gentleman gives him out to be of good capacity and breeding; his employment between his lord and my niece confirms no less: therefore this letter, being so excellently ignorant, will breed no terror in the youth: he will find it comes from a clodpole. But, sir, I will deliver his challenge by word of mouth; set upon Aguecheek a notable report of valor, and drive the gentleman, as I know his youth will aptly receive it, into a most hideous opinion of his rage, skill, fury, and impetuosity. This will so fright them both that they will kill one another by the look, like cockatrices.[2]

---

[1] Bum or bound bailiff is analogous to our sheriff's deputy.

[2] The cockatrice, a fabulous animal, with the head of a cock, the wings of a fowl, and the tail of a dragon, was supposed to have the power of killing with a glance of the eye.

Fabian. Here he comes with your niece: give them way till he take leave, and presently after him.

Sir Toby. I will meditate the while upon some horrid message for a challenge.   [*Exeunt Sir Toby, Fabian, and Maria.*

Olivia. I have said too much unto a heart of stone
And laid mine honor too unchary out:
There's something in me that reproves my fault;
But such a headstrong potent fault it is,
That it but mocks reproof.

Viola. With the same 'havior that your passion bears
Goes on my master's grief.

Olivia. Here, wear this jewel for me, 'tis my picture;
Refuse it not; it hath no tongue to vex you;
And I beseech you come again to-morrow.
What shall you ask of me that I'll deny,
That honor sav'd may upon asking give?

Viola. Nothing but this; your true love for my master.

Olivia. How with mine honor may I give him that
Which I have given to you?

Viola.   I will acquit you.

Olivia. Well, come again to-morrow: fare thee well:
A fiend like thee might bear my soul to hell.   [*Exit.*

Sir Toby. Gentleman, God save thee.

Viola. And you, sir.

Sir Toby. That defense thou hast, betake thee to't: of what nature the wrongs are thou hast done him, I know not; but thy intercepter, full of despite, bloody as the hunter, attends thee at the orchard-end: dismount thy tuck, be yare[1] in thy preparation, for thy assailant is quick, skillful and deadly.

---

[1] "Dismount thy tuck," etc., i.e., unsheath thy rapier; be ready.

Viola. You mistake, sir; I am sure no man hath any quarrel to me: my remembrance is very free and clear from any image of offense done to any man.

Sir Toby. You'll find it otherwise, I assure you: therefore, if you hold your life at any price, betake you to your guard; for your opposite hath in him what youth, strength, skill and wrath can furnish man withal.

Viola. I pray you, sir, what is he?

Sir Toby. He is knight, dubb'd with unhack'd rapier and on carpet consideration; but he is a devil in private brawl: souls and bodies hath he divorc'd three; and his incensement at this moment is so implacable, that satisfaction can be none but by pangs of death and sepulcher. Hobnob is his word; give't or take't.

Viola. I will return again into the house and desire some conduct[1] of the lady. I am no fighter. I have heard of some kind of men that put quarrels purposely on others, to taste[2] their valor: belike this is a man of that quirk.[3]

Sir Toby. Sir, no; his indignation derives itself out of a very competent injury: therefore, get you on and give him his desire. Back you shall not to the house, unless you undertake that with me which with as much safety you might answer him: therefore, on, or strip your sword stark naked; for meddle you must, that's certain, or forswear to wear iron about you.

Viola. This is as uncivil as strange. I beseech you, do me this courteous office, as to know of the knight what my offense to him is: it is something of my negligence, nothing of my purpose.

Sir Toby. I will do so. Signior Fabian, stay you by this gentleman till my return.　　　　　　　　　　　　　　　[*Exit.*

Viola. Pray you, sir, do you know of this matter?

Fabian. I know the knight is incens'd against you, even to a mortal arbitrament; but nothing of the circumstance more.

Viola. I beseech you, what manner of man is he?

---

[1] Escort.　　　　　　[2] Test.　　　　　　[3] Whim.

Fabian. Nothing of that wonderful promise, to read him by his form, as you are like to find him in the proof of his valor. He is, indeed, sir, the most skillful, bloody and fatal opposite that you could possibly have found in any part of Illyria. Will you walk towards him? I will make your peace with him if I can.

Viola. I shall be much bound to you for't: I am one that had rather go with sir priest than sir knight: I care not who knows so much of my mettle.   [*Exeunt.*

Reënter SIR TOBY, *with* SIR ANDREW.

Sir Toby. Why, man, he's a very devil; I have not seen such a firago.[1] I had a pass with him, rapier, scabbard and all, and he gives me the stuck in with such a mortal motion, that it is inevitable;[2] and on the answer, he pays you as surely as your feet hit the ground they step on. They say he has been fencer to the Sophy.

Sir Andrew. I'll not meddle with him.

Sir Toby. Ay, but he will not now be pacified: Fabian can scarce hold him yonder.

Sir Andrew. Plague on't, an I thought he had been valiant and so cunning in fence, I'ld have seen him damn'd ere I'ld have challeng'd him. Let him let the matter slip, and I'll give him my horse, gray Capilet.

Sir Toby. I'll make the motion: stand here, make a good show on't: this shall end without the perdition of souls. [*Aside*] Marry, I'll ride your horse as well as I ride you.

Reënter FABIAN *and* VIOLA.

[*To Fabian*] I have his horse to take up the quarrel: I have persuaded him the youth's a devil.

Fabian. He is as horribly conceited of him; and pants and looks pale, as if a bear were at his heels.

---

1 Sir Toby means " virago."

2 " The stuck in with," etc., i.e., it is impossible to parry the deadly precision of his thrust.

Sir Toby. [*To Viola*] There's no remedy, sir; he will fight with you for's oath sake: marry, he had better bethought him of his quarrel, and he finds that now scarce to be worth talking of: therefore draw, for the supportance of his vow; he protests he will not hurt you.

Viola. [*Aside*] Pray God defend me! A little thing would make me tell them how much I lack of a man.

Fabian. Give ground, if you see him furious.

Sir Toby. Come, Sir Andrew, there's no remedy; the gentleman will, for his honor's sake, have one bout with you; he cannot by the duello[1] avoid it: but he has promis'd me, as he is a gentleman and a soldier, he will not hurt you. Come on; to't.

Sir Andrew. Pray God, he keep his oath!

Viola. I do assure you, 'tis against my will.   [*They draw.*

Enter ANTONIO.

Antonio. Put up your sword. If this young gentleman
Have done offense, I take the fault on me:
If you offend him, I for him defy you.

Sir Toby. You, sir! why, what are you?

Antonio. One, sir, that for his love dares yet do more
Than you have heard him brag to you he will.

Sir Toby. Nay, if you be an undertaker,[2] I am for you.
    [*They draw.*

Enter Officers.

Fabian. O good Sir Toby, hold! here come the officers.

Sir Toby. I'll be with you anon.

Viola. Pray, sir, put your sword up, if you please.

Sir Andrew. Marry, will I, sir; and, for that I promis'd you, I'll be as good as my word: he will bear you easily and reins well.

---

[1] The laws that regulate dueling.
[2] Here used in the sense of an intermeddler.

First Officer. This is the man; do thy office.

Second Officer. Antonio, I arrest thee at the suit of Count
Orsino.

Antonio. You do mistake me, sir.

First Officer. No, sir, no jot; I know your favor well,
Though now you have no sea-cap on your head.
Take him away: he knows I know him well.

    Antonio. I .must obey. [*To Viola*] This comes with seeking
      you:
But there's no remedy; I shall answer it.
What will you do, now my necessity
Makes me to ask you for my purse?   It grieves me
Much more for what I cannot do for you
Than what befalls myself.   You stand amaz'd;
But be of comfort.

    Second Officer. Come, sir, away.

    Antonio. I must entreat of you some of that money.

    Viola. What money, sir?
For the fair kindness you have show'd me here,
And, part, being prompted by your present trouble,
Out of my lean and low ability
I'll lend you something: my having is not much;
I'll make division of my present[1] with you:
Hold, there's half my coffer.

    Antonio.   Will you deny me now?
Is't possible that my deserts to you
Can lack persuasion?   Do not tempt my misery,
Lest that it make me so unsound a man
As to upbraid you with those kindnesses
That I have done for you.

    Viola.   I know of none;
Nor know I you by voice or any feature:
I hate ingratitude more in a man
Than lying, vainness, babbling, drunkenness,

---

[1] Present store.

Or any taint of vice whose strong corruption
Inhabits our frail blood.

Antonio.   O heavens themselves!

Second Officer. Come, sir, I pray you, go.

Antonio. Let me speak a little. This youth that you see here
I snatch'd one half out of the jaws of death;
Reliev'd him with such sanctity of love;
And to his image, which methought did promise
Most venerable worth, did I devotion.

First Officer. What's that to us? The time goes by: away!

Antonio. But O how vile an idol proves this god!
Thou hast, Sebastian, done good feature shame.
In nature there's no blemish but the mind;
None can be call'd deform'd but the unkind:
Virtue is beauty, but the beauteous evil
Are empty trunks o'erflourish'd[1] by the devil.

First Officer. The man grows mad: away with him! Come,
come, sir.

Antonio. Lead me on.   [*Exit with officers.*

Viola. Methinks his words do from such passion fly,
That he believes himself: so do not I.[2]
Prove true, imagination, O, prove true,
That I, dear brother, be now ta'en for you!

Sir Toby. Come hither, knight; come hither, Fabian: we'll
whisper o'er a couplet or two of most sage saws.

Viola. He named Sebastian: I my brother know
Yet living in my glass;[3] even such and so
In favor was my brother, and he went
Still in this fashion, color, ornament,

---

[1] Trunks and chests, being articles of furniture, were often richly orna-
mented with carvings.

[2] "So do not I," i.e., I do not yet believe myself, when from this
accident I gather hope of my brother's life.

[3] "I my brother know," etc., i.e., I see my brother as if living in my own
reflection in the glass.

For him I imitate :[1] O, if it prove,
Tempests are kind and salt waves fresh in love.   [*Exit.*

Sir Toby. A very dishonest paltry boy, and more a coward than a hare: his dishonesty appears in leaving his friend here in necessity and denying him; and for his cowardship, ask Fabian.

Fabian. A coward, a most devout coward, religious in it.

Sir Andrew. 'Slid, I'll after him again and beat him.

Sir Toby. Do; cuff him soundly, but never draw thy sword.

Sir Andrew. An I do not —   [*Exit.*

Fabian. Come, let's see the event.

Sir Toby. I dare lay any money 'twill be nothing yet.   .
    [*Exeunt.*

ACT IV.

SCENE I. *Before Olivia's House.*

Enter SEBASTIAN *and* CLOWN.

Clown. Will you make me believe that I am not sent for you?

Sebastian. Go to, go to, thou art a foolish fellow:
Let me be clear of thee.

Clown. Well held out, i' faith! No, I do not know you; nor I am not sent to you by my lady, to bid you come speak with her; nor your name is not Master Cesario; nor this is not my nose neither. Nothing that is so is so.

Sebastian. I prithee, vent thy folly somewhere else:
Thou know'st not me.

Clown. Vent my folly! he has heard that word of some great man and now applies it to a fool. Vent my folly! I am afraid this great lubber, the world, will prove a cockney. I prithee now, ungird thy strangeness,[2] and tell me what I shall vent to my lady: shall I vent to her that thou art coming?

---

[1] "He went still," etc., i.e., I imitate his dress in fashion, color, and ornament.

[2] "Ungird thy strangeness," i.e., put off thy pretense of not knowing me.

Sebastian. I prithee, foolish Greek,[1] depart from me:
There's money for thee: if you tarry longer,
I shall give worse payment.

Clown. By my troth, thou hast an open hand. These wise
men that give fools money get themselves a good report — after
fourteen years' purchase.

Enter SIR ANDREW, SIR TOBY, *and* FABIAN.

Sir Andrew. Now, sir, have I met you again? there's for you.

Sebastian. Why, there's for thee, and there, and there.
Are all the people mad?

Sir Toby. Hold, sir, or I'll throw your dagger o'er the house.

Clown. This will I tell my lady straight: I would not be in
some of your coats for twopence.   [*Exit.*

Sir Toby. Come on, sir; hold.

Sir Andrew. Nay, let him alone: I'll go another way to work
with him; I'll have an action of battery against him, if there be
any law in Illyria: though I struck him first, yet it's no matter
for that.

Sebastian. Let go thy hand.

Sir Toby. Come, sir, I will not let you go. Come, my young
soldier, put up your iron: you are well flesh'd; come on.[2]

Sebastian. I will[3] be free from thee. What wouldst thou now?
If thou dar'st tempt me further, draw thy sword.

Sir Toby. What, what? Nay, then I must have an ounce or
two of this malapert blood from you.

Enter OLIVIA.

Olivia. Hold, Toby; on thy life I charge thee, hold!

Sir Toby. Madam!

---

1 " Foolish Greek," i.e., foolish jester; " as merry as a Greek " was
proverbial.

2 " Put up your iron," etc., i.e., put up your sword; you are eager to use
it for one so young: come away.

3 Wish to.

Olivia. Will it be ever thus? Ungracious wretch,
Fit for the mountains and the barbarous caves,
Where manners ne'er were preach'd! out of my sight!
Be not offended, dear Cesario.
Rudesby,[1] be gone! [*Exeunt Sir Toby, Sir Andrew, and Fabian.*
I prithee, gentle friend,
Let thy fair wisdom, not thy passion, sway
In this uncivil and unjust extent[2]
Against thy peace. Go with me to my house,
And hear thou there how many fruitless pranks
This ruffian hath botch'd up, that thou thereby
Mayst smile at this: thou shalt not choose but go:
Do not deny. Beshrew his soul for me,
He started one poor heart[3] of mine in thee.
Sebastian. What relish is in this? how runs the stream?
Or I am mad, or else this is a dream:
Let fancy still my sense in Lethe[4] steep;
If it be thus to dream, still let me sleep!
Olivia. Nay, come, I prithee; would thou'ldst be rul'd by me!
Sebastian. Madam, I will.
Olivia. O, say so, and so be! [*Exeunt.*

SCENE II. *Olivia's House.*

Enter MARIA *and* CLOWN.

Maria. Nay, I prithee, put on this gown and this beard; make him believe thou art Sir Topas the curate: do it quickly; I'll call Sir Toby the whilst. [*Exit.*

---

[1] Rude fellow.
[2] "Extent" is an English common-law writ of execution whereby goods are seized for the King. It is therefore taken here for violence in general.
[3] Olivia, using "started" in the sense of starting game, puns on "heart" and "hart."
[4] In classical mythology, one of the rivers of Hades, the waters of which had the effect of making those who drank them forget what they had done, heard, or seen before.

Clown. Well, I'll put it on, and I will dissemble myself in't; and I would I were the first that ever dissembled in such a gown. I am not tall enough to become the function well, nor lean enough to be thought a good student; but to be said an honest man and a good housekeeper goes as fairly as to say a careful man and a great scholar. The competitors[1] enter.

Enter SIR TOBY *and* MARIA.

Sir Toby. Jove bless thee, Master Parson.

Clown. Bonos dies,[2] Sir Toby: for, as the old hermit of Prague,[3] that never saw pen and ink, very wittily said to a niece of King Gorboduc, "That that is, is;" so I, being Master Parson, am Master Parson; for what is "that" but "that," and "is" but "is"?

Sir Toby. To him, Sir Topas.

Clown. What, ho, I say! peace in this prison!

Sir Toby. The knave counterfeits well; a good knave.

Malvolio. [*Within*] Who calls there?

Clown. Sir Topas the curate, who comes to visit Malvolio the lunatic.

Malvolio. Sir Topas, Sir Topas, good Sir Topas, go to my lady.

Clown. Out, hyperbolical fiend! how vexest thou this man! talkest thou nothing but of ladies?

Sir Toby. Well said, Master Parson.

Malvolio. Sir Topas, never was man thus wronged: good Sir Topas, do not think I am mad: they have laid me here in hideous darkness.

Clown. Fie, thou dishonest Satan! I call thee by the most modest terms; for I am one of those gentle ones that will use the devil himself with courtesy: say'st thou that house is dark?

---

1 Confederates.   2 Happy days, good day.

3 This hermit and the niece of King Gorboduc, and probably Gorboduc, are creations of the inventive clown.

Malvolio. As hell, Sir Topas.

Clown. Why, it hath bay windows transparent as barricadoes, and the clearstories toward the south north are as lustrous as ebony; and yet complainest thou of obstruction?

Malvolio. I am not mad, Sir Topas: I say to you, this house is dark.

Clown. Madman, thou errest: I say, there is no darkness but ignorance; in which thou art more puzzl'd than the Egyptians in their fog.[1]

Malvolio. I say, this house is as dark as ignorance, though ignorance were as dark as hell; and I say, there was never man thus abus'd. I am no more mad than you are: make the trial of it in any constant question.

Clown. What is the opinion of Pythagoras[2] concerning wild fowl?

Malvolio. That the soul of our grandam might haply inhabit a bird.

Clown. What think'st thou of his opinion?

Malvolio. I think nobly of the soul, and no way approve his opinion.

Clown. Fare thee well. Remain thou still in darkness: thou shalt hold the opinion of Pythagoras ere I will allow of thy wits, and fear to kill a woodcock, lest thou dispossess the soul of thy grandam. Fare thee well.

Malvolio. Sir Topas, Sir Topas!

Sir Toby. My most exquisite Sir Topas!

Clown. Nay, I am for all waters.[3]

Maria. Thou mightst have done this without thy beard and gown: he sees thee not.

Sir Toby. To him in thine own voice, and bring me word how

---

[1] See Exodus x. 21, 22.

[2] This celebrated Greek philosopher, one of whose doctrines was the transmigration of souls, flourished about five hundred years before the Christian era.

[3] " Nay, I am," etc., i.e., Oh, I can turn my hand to anything.

thou find'st him: I would we were well rid of this knavery. If he may be conveniently deliver'd, I would he were, for I am now so far in offense with my niece that I cannot pursue with any safety this sport to the upshot. Come by and by to my chamber. [*Exeunt Sir Toby and Maria.*

Clown. [*Singing*] "*Hey, Robin, jolly Robin,*
    Tell me how thy lady does."

Malvolio. Fool!

Clown. "My lady is unkind, perdy."

Malvolio. Fool!

Clown. "Alas, why is she so?"

Malvolio. Fool, I say!

Clown. "She loves another" — Who calls, ha?

Malvolio. Good fool, as ever thou wilt deserve well at my hand, help me to a candle, and pen, ink and paper: as I am a gentleman, I will live to be thankful to thee for't.

Clown. Master Malvolio?

Malvolio. Ay, good fool.

Clown. Alas, sir, how fell you beside your five wits?

Malvolio. Fool, there was never man so notoriously abus'd: I am as well in my wits, fool, as thou art.

Clown. But as well? then you are mad, indeed, if you be no better in your wits than a fool.

Malvolio. They have here propertied me;[1] keep me in darkness, send ministers to me, asses, and do all they can to face me out of my wits.

Clown. Advise you what you say; the minister is here.[2] Malvolio, Malvolio, thy wits the heavens restore! endeavor thyself to sleep, and leave thy vain bibble babble.

Malvolio. Sir Topas!

---

[1] "Propertied me," i.e., made a property of me; treated me as if I had no will of my own.

[2] The clown, in this speech and his next, acts two persons, counterfeiting by variation of voice a conversation between the curate and himself, and an exhortation of the former to Malvolio.

Clown. Maintain no words with him, good fellow. Who, I, sir? not I, sir. God be wi' you, good Sir Topas. Marry, amen. I will, sir, I will.

Malvolio. Fool, fool, fool, I say!

Clown. Alas, sir, be patient. What say you, sir? I am shent[1] for speaking to you.

Malvolio. Good fool, help me to some light and some paper: I tell thee, I am as well in my wits as any man in Illyria.

Clown. Well-a-day that you were, sir!

Malvolio. By this hand, I am. Good fool, some ink, paper and light; and convey what I will set down to my lady: it shall advantage thee more than ever the bearing of letter did.

Clown. I will help you to't. But tell me true, are you not mad indeed? or do you but counterfeit?

Malvolio. Believe me, I am not; I tell thee true.

Clown. Nay, I'll ne'er believe a madman till I see his brains. I will fetch you light and paper and ink.

Malvolio. Fool, I'll requite it in the highest degree: I prithee, be gone.

Clown. [*Singing*] *I am gone, sir,*
                            And anon, sir,
                I'll be with you again,
                    In a trice,
                    Like to the old Vice,[2]
                    Your need to sustain;

                Who, with dagger of lath,
                In his rage and his wrath,
                    Cries, ah, ha! to the devil:
                Like a mad lad,
                Pare thy nails, dad;
                    Adieu, good man devil.   [*Exit.*

[1] Scolded.

[2] Vice was one of the characters in the Moralities, or Moral plays, which were common a century before Shakespeare's time. In them the performers personated such characters as Mercy, Virtue, Vice, etc. This last character, who always appeared accompanied by the Devil, played all manner of

Scene III. *Olivia's Garden.*

Enter Sebastian.

Sebastian. This is the air; that is the glorious sun;
This pearl she gave me, I do feel't and see't;
And though 'tis wonder that inwraps me thus,
Yet 'tis not madness. Where's Antonio, then?
I could not find him at the Elephant:
Yet there he was; and there I found this credit,[1]
That he did range the town to seek me out.
His counsel now might do me golden service;
For though my soul disputes well with my sense,
That this may be some error, but no madness,
Yet doth this accident and flood of fortune
So far exceed all instance, all discourse,[2]
That I am ready to distrust mine eyes
And wrangle with my reason that persuades me
To any other trust but that I am mad
Or else the lady's mad; yet, if 'twere so,
She could not sway her house, command her followers,
Take and give back affairs and their dispatch[3]
With such a smooth, discreet and stable bearing
As I perceive she does: there's something in't
That is deceivable. But here the lady comes.

Enter Olivia *and* Priest.

Olivia. Blame not this haste of mine. If you mean well,
Now go with me and with this holy man

practical jokes on him, mounting his back, beating his sides with a sword of
lath, cutting his long nails with a wooden dagger, etc., greatly to the amuse-
ment of the spectators.

1 News or intelligence.

2 " All instance, all discourse," i.e., all example, all reason.

3 " Take and give back," etc., i.e., take in hand and discharge matters
of business.

Into the chantry[1] by: there, before him,
And underneath that consecrated roof,
Plight me[2] the full assurance of your faith;
That my most jealous and too doubtful[3] soul
May live at peace.   He shall conceal it
Whiles you are willing it shall come to note,
What time we will our celebration keep
According to my birth.[4]   What do you say?
   Sebastian.   I'll follow this good man, and go with you;
And, having sworn truth, ever will be true.
   Olivia.   Then lead the way, good father; and heavens so shine,
That they may fairly note this act of mine!   [*Exeunt.*

ACT V.

SCENE I.   *Before Olivia's House.*

Enter CLOWN *and* FABIAN.

Fabian.   Now, as thou lov'st me, let me see his letter.
Clown.   Good Master Fabian, grant me another request.
Fabian.   Anything.
Clown.   Do not desire to see this letter.
Fabian.   This is, to give a dog, and in recompense desire my
dog again.

Enter DUKE, VIOLA, CURIO, *and* Lords.

Duke.   Belong you to the Lady Olivia, friends?
Clown.   Ay, sir; we are some of her trappings.
Duke.   I know thee well: how dost thou, my good fellow?

---

[1] A private chapel.
[2] " Plight me," etc.   This was a betrothal, not a full marriage ceremony.
[3] Fearful.
[4] " Whiles you are willing," etc., i.e., until you are willing it shall be
made known : we will then celebrate our nuptials in a manner befitting my
social position.

Clown. Truly, sir, the better for my foes and the worse for my friends.

Duke. Just the contrary; the better for thy friends.

Clown. No, sir, the worse.

Duke. How can that be?

Clown. Marry, sir, they praise me and make an ass of me; now my foes tell me plainly I am an ass: so that by my foes, sir, I profit in the knowledge of myself, and by my friends I am abus'd: so that, conclusions to be as kisses, if your four negatives make your two affirmatives, why then, the worse for my friends and the better for my foes.

Duke. Why, this is excellent.

Clown. By my troth, sir, no; though it please you to be one of my friends.

Duke. Thou shalt not be the worse for me: there's gold.

Clown. But that it would be double-dealing, sir, I would you could make it another.

Duke. O, you give me ill counsel.

Clown. Put your grace in your pocket, sir, for this once, and let your flesh and blood obey it.

Duke. Well, I will be so much a sinner, to be a double-dealer: there's another.

Clown. Primo, secundo, tertio, is a good play; and the old saying is, the third pays for all: the triplex, sir, is a good tripping measure; or[1] the bells of Saint Bennet, sir, may put you in mind; one, two, three.

Duke. You can fool no more money out of me at this throw: if you will let your lady know I am here to speak with her, and bring her along with you, it may awake my bounty further.

Clown. Marry, sir, lullaby to your bounty till I come again. I go, sir; but I would not have you to think that my desire of having is the sin of covetousness: but, as you say, sir, let your bounty take a nap, I will awake it anon.   [*Exit.*

Viola. Here comes the man, sir, that did rescue me.

---

[1] As.

Enter ANTONIO *and* Officers.

Duke. That face of his I do remember well;
Yet, when I saw it last, it was besmear'd
As black as Vulcan[1] in the smoke of war:
A bawbling[2] vessel was he captain of,
For shallow draught and bulk unprizable;[3]
With which such scathful grapple did he make
With the most noble bottom[4] of our fleet,
That very envy and the tongue of loss[5]
Cried fame and honor on him. What's the matter?

First Officer. Orsino, this is that Antonio
That took the Phœnix and her fraught from Candy;[6]
And this is he that did the Tiger board,
When your young nephew Titus lost his leg:
Here in the streets, desperate of shame and state,[7]
In private brabble did we apprehend him.

Viola. He did me kindness, sir, drew[8] on my side;
But in conclusion put strange speech upon me:
I know not what 'twas but distraction.[9]

Duke. Notable pirate! thou salt-water thief!
What foolish boldness brought thee to their mercies,
Whom thou, in terms so bloody and so dear,[10]
Hast made thine enemies?

Antonio.   Orsino, noble sir,
Be pleas'd that I shake off these names you give me:

---

[1] The smith who forged armor for the gods of the Greek mythology.
[2] Insignificant.   [3] Worthless.   [4] Ship.   [5] The losers.
[6] " Fraught from Candy," i.e., her freight when coming from Candia.
[7] " Desperate of shame," etc., i.e., utterly regardless of shame and danger.
[8] Drew his sword.
[9] " Put strange speech," etc., i.e., said strange things to me: I know not why he did it, save that he is mad.
[10] " Dear " is often used by Shakespeare as a term of intensity, whether of love or hate.

Antonio never yet was thief or pirate,
Though I confess, on base and ground enough,
Orsino's enemy.   A witchcraft drew me hither:
That most ingrateful boy there by your side,
From the rude sea's enrag'd and foamy mouth
Did I redeem; a wreck past hope he was:
His life I gave him and did thereto add
My love, without retention or restraint,
All his in dedication; for his sake
Did I expose myself, pure for his love,
Into the danger of this adverse town;
Drew to defend him when he was beset:
Where being apprehended, his false cunning,
Not meaning to partake with me in danger,
Taught him to face me out of his acquaintance,
And grew a twenty years removed thing
While one would wink; deni'd me mine own purse,
Which I had recommended[1] to his use
Not half an hour before.

    Viola.   How can this be?

    Duke. When came he to this town?

    Antonio. To-day, my lord; and for three months before,
No interim, not a minute's vacancy,
Both day and night did we keep company.

Enter OLIVIA *and* Attendants.

    Duke. Here comes the countess: now heaven walks on earth.
But for thee, fellow; fellow, thy words are madness:
Three months this youth hath tended upon me;
But more of that anon.   Take him aside.

    Olivia. What would my lord, but that he may not have,
Wherein Olivia may seem serviceable?
Cesario, you do not keep promise with me.

---

[1] Intrusted.

Viola. Madam!

Duke. Gracious Olivia—

Olivia. What do you say, Cesario?   Good my lord—

Viola. My lord would speak; my duty hushes me.

Olivia. If it be aught to the old tune, my lord,
It is as fat and fulsome[1] to mine ear
As howling after music.

Duke.   Still so cruel?

Olivia. Still so constant, lord.

Duke. What, to perverseness? you uncivil lady,
To whose ingrate and unauspicious altars
My soul the faithful'st offerings hath breath'd out
That e'er devotion tender'd!   What shall I do?

Olivia. Even what it please my lord, that shall become him.

Duke. Why should I not, had I the heart to do it,
Like to the Egyptian thief[2] at point of death,
Kill what I love? — a savage jealousy
That sometimes savors nobly.   But hear me this:
Since you to non-regardance cast my faith,
And that I partly know the instrument
That screws me from my true place in your favor,
Live you the marble-breasted tyrant still;
But this your minion, whom I know you love,
And whom, by heaven I swear, I tender dearly,
Him will I tear out of that cruel eye,
Where he sits crowned in his master's spite.
Come, boy, with me; my thoughts are ripe in mischief:
I'll sacrifice the lamb that I do love,
To spite a raven's heart within a dove.

---

[1] " Fat and fulsome," i.e., cloying and sickening.

[2] The story alluded to is found in Heliodorus's Æthiopica: Thyamis, a native of Memphis, at the head of a band of robbers, had seized Theagenes and Charicleia, and had fallen in love with the latter.   Being attacked by another company of robbers, he shut her up in a cave with his treasures, until, despairing of safety, he attempted to murder her.

Viola. And I, most jocund, apt and willingly,
To do you rest,[1] a thousand deaths would die.
Olivia. Where goes Cesario?
·*Viola.*   After him I love
More than I love these eyes, more than my life,
More, by all mores, than e'er I shall love wife.
If I do feign, you witnesses above
Punish my life for tainting of my love!
Olivia. Ay me, detested! how am I beguiled!
Viola. Who does beguile you? who does do you wrong?
Olivia. Hast thou forgot thyself? is it so long?
Call forth the holy father.   [*Attendant goes out.*
Duke.   Come, away!
Olivia. Whither, my lord? Cesario, husband, stay.
Duke. Husband!
Olivia.   Ay, husband: can he that deny?
Duke. Her husband, sirrah!
Viola.   No, my lord, not I.
Olivia. Alas, it is the baseness of thy fear
That makes thee strangle thy propriety:[2]
Fear not, Cesario; take thy fortunes up;
Be that thou know'st thou art, and then thou art
As great as that thou fear'st.

Enter Attendant *and* Priest.

                    O, welcome, father!
Father, I charge thee, by thy reverence,
Here to unfold, though lately we intended
To keep in darkness what occasion now
Reveals before 'tis ripe, what thou dost know
Hath newly pass'd between this youth and me.
Priest. A contract of eternal bond of love,
Confirm'd by mutual joinder of your hands,

---

1 " To do you rest," i.e., to give you ease.
2 " Strangle thy propriety," i.e., deny thy proper self or identity.

Attested by the holy close of lips,
Strengthen'd by interchangement of your rings;
And all the ceremony of this compact
Seal'd in my function, by my testimony:
Since when, my watch hath told me, toward my grave
I have travel'd but two hours.

Duke. O thou dissembling cub! what wilt thou be
When time hath sow'd a grizzle on thy case?[1]
Or will not else thy craft so quickly grow,
That thine own trip shall be thine overthrow?[2]
Farewell, and take her; but direct thy feet
Where thou and I henceforth may never meet.

Viola. My lord, I do protest —
Olivia.   O, do not swear!
Hold little faith, though thou hast too much fear.

Enter SIR ANDREW.

Sir Andrew. For the love of God, a surgeon! Send one presently to Sir Toby.

Olivia. What's the matter?

Sir Andrew. He has broke my head across and has given Sir Toby a bloody coxcomb too: for the love of God, your help! I had rather than forty pound I were at home.

Olivia. Who has done this, Sir Andrew?

Sir Andrew. The count's gentleman, one Cesario: we took him for a coward, but he's the very devil incardinate.

Duke. My gentleman, Cesario?

Sir Andrew. 'Od's lifelings, here he is! You broke my head for nothing; and that that I did, I was set on to do't by Sir Toby.

Viola. Why do you speak to me? I never hurt you:

---

[1] " Case " was the technical name for " skin," of furred animals especially.

[2] " That thine own trip," etc., i.e., that you may be caught in your own snare.

You drew your sword upon me without cause;
But I bespake you fair, and hurt you not.

Sir Andrew. If a bloody coxcomb be a hurt, you have hurt
me: I think you set nothing by a bloody coxcomb.

Enter SIR TOBY *and* CLOWN.

Here comes Sir Toby halting; you shall hear more: but if he
had not been in drink, he would have tickled you othergates[1]
than he did.

Duke. How now, gentleman! how is't with you?

Sir Toby. That's all one: 'has hurt me, and there's the end
on't. Sot, didst see Dick surgeon, sot?

Clown. O, he's drunk, Sir Toby, an hour agone; his eyes
were set at eight i' the morning.

Sir Toby. Then he's a rogue, and a passy-measures panym:[2]
I hate a drunken rogue.

Olivia. Away with him! Who hath made this havoc with
them?

Sir Andrew. I'll help you, Sir Toby, because we'll be dress'd
together.

Sir Toby. Will you help? an ass-head and a coxcomb and a
knave, a thin-fac'd knave, a gull!

Olivia. Get him to bed, and let his hurt be look'd to.

[Exeunt Clown, Fabian, Sir Toby, and Sir Andrew.

Enter SEBASTIAN.

Sebastian. I am sorry, madam, I have hurt your kinsman;
But, had it been the brother of my blood,
I must have done no less with wit and safety.
You throw a strange regard upon me, and by that

---

[1] In another manner.

[2] "A rogue, and a passy-measures panym." Sir Toby is very deep in
his cups, and his tongue is thick. He tries to call the surgeon "a *past-
measure panym*" or pagan. "Pagan" and "heathen" were common terms
of reproach.

I do perceive it hath offended you :
Pardon me, sweet one, even for the vows
We made each other but so late ago.

Duke. One face, one voice, one habit, and two persons,
A natural perspective,[1] that is and is not!

Sebastian. Antonio, O my dear Antonio!
How have the hours rack'd and tortur'd me,
Since I have lost thee!

Antonio. Sebastian are you?

Sebastian.   Fear'st thou that, Antonio?

Antonio. How have you made division of yourself?
An apple, cleft in two, is not more twin
Than these two creatures. Which is Sebastian?

Olivia. Most wonderful.

Sebastian. Do I stand there? I never had a brother;
Nor can there be that deity in my nature,
Of here and everywhere.[2] I had a sister,
Whom the blind waves and surges have devour'd.
Of charity,[3] what kin are you to me?
What countryman? what name? what parentage?

Viola. Of Messaline : Sebastian was my father;
Such a Sebastian was my brother too,
So went he suited[4] to his watery tomb :
If spirits can assume both form and suit,
You come to fright us.

Sebastian.   A spirit I am indeed;
But am in that dimension grossly clad

---

[1] " It is a pretty art that in a pleated paper and table framed or indented, men make one picture to represent several faces,— which being viewed from one place or standing did show the head of a Spaniard, and from another the head of an ass." Pictures so arranged are common nowadays as advertising signs.

[2] " Deity in my nature," etc., i.e., godlike attribute in my nature of being here and elsewhere at the same time.

[3] " Of charity," i.e., in kindness tell me.

[4] " So went he," etc., i.e., he went, dressed as you are.

Which from my birth I did participate.[1]
Were you a woman, as the rest goes even,
I should my tears let fall upon your cheek,
And say " Thrice-welcome, drowned Viola! "
    Viola. My father had a mole upon his brow.
    Sebastian. And so had mine.
    Viola. And died that day when Viola from her birth
Had number'd thirteen years.
    Sebastian. O, that record is lively in my soul!
He finished indeed his mortal act
That day that made my sister thirteen years.
    Viola. If nothing lets[2] to make us happy both
But this my masculine usurp'd attire,
Do not embrace me till each circumstance
Of place, time, fortune, do cohere and jump[3]
That I am Viola: which to confirm,
I'll bring you to a captain in this town,
Where lie my maiden weeds ;[4] by whose gentle help
I was preserv'd to serve this noble count.
All the occurrence of my fortune since
Hath been between this lady and this lord.
    Sebastian. [*To Olivia*] So comes it, lady, you have been
        mistook :[5]
But nature to her bias drew in that.
You would have been contracted to a maid ;
Nor are you therein, by my life, deceiv'd,
You are betroth'd both to a maid and man.
    Duke. Be not amaz'd ; right noble is his blood.
If this be so, as yet the glass seems true,
I shall have share in this most happy wreck.
[*To Viola*] Boy, thou hast said to me a thousand times
Thou never shouldst love woman like to me.

---

1 " But am in that dimension," etc., i.e., but am clad in that same gross
body which I did receive at my birth.
  2 Hinders.   3 Agree.   4 Clothes.   5 Mistaken.

Viola. And all those sayings will I over-swear;
And all those swearings keep as true in soul
As doth that orbed continent the fire
That severs day from night.
Duke.   Give me thy hand;
And let me see thee in thy woman's weeds.
Viola. The captain that did bring me first on shore
Hath my maid's garments: he upon some action
Is now in durance, at Malvolio's suit,
A gentleman, and follower of my lady's.
Olivia. He shall enlarge him: fetch Malvolio hither:
And yet, alas, now I remember me,
They say, poor gentleman, he's much distract.

Reënter CLOWN *with a letter, and* FABIAN.

A most extracting frenzy[1] of mine own
From my remembrance clearly banish'd his.
How does he, sirrah?
Clown. Truly, madam, he holds Belzebub at the stave's end
as well as a man in his case may do: 'has here writ a letter to
you; I should have given't you to-day morning, but as a mad-
man's epistles are no gospels, so it skills[2] not much when they
are deliver'd.
Olivia. Open't, and read it.
Clown. Look then to be well edified when the fool delivers
the madman. [*Reads*] "*By the Lord, madam*" —
Olivia. How now! art thou mad?
Clown. No, madam, I do but read madness: an your ladyship
will have it as it ought to be, you must allow Vox.[3]

---

[1] Olivia alludes to her passion for Cesario as an *extracting* frenzy, since it
effaced from her remembrance her steward's supposed lunacy.

[2] Matters.

[3] " An your ladyship," etc. This is Malone's explanation: " If you
would have it read in character, as such a mad epistle ought to be, you must
permit me to assume a frantic tone." Vox is equivalent to voice.

Olivia. Prithee, read i' thy right wits.

Clown. So I do, madonna; but to read his right wits is to read thus: therefore perpend,[1] my princess, and give ear.

Olivia. Read it you, sirrah. 　　　　　　　　　　[*To Fabian.*

Fabian. [*Reads*] "*By the Lord, madam, you wrong me, and the world shall know it: though you have put me into darkness and given your drunken cousin rule over me, yet have I the benefit of my senses as well as your ladyship. I have your own letter that induced me to the semblance I put on; with the which I doubt not but to do myself much right, or you much shame. Think of me as you please. I leave my duty a little unthought of and speak out of my injury.*

　　　　　　　　　　　　　"THE MADLY-USED MALVOLIO."

Olivia. Did he write this?

Clown. Ay, madam.

Duke. This savors not much of distraction.

Olivia. See him deliver'd, Fabian; bring him hither.

　　　　　　　　　　　　　　　　　[*Exit Fabian.*

My lord, so please you, these things further thought on,

To think me as well a sister as a wife,

One day shall crown th' alliance on't, so please you,

Here at my house and at my proper cost.[2]

Duke. Madam, I am most apt to embrace your offer.

[*To Viola*] Your master quits[3] you; and for your service done

　　　him,

So much against the mettle of your sex,

So far beneath your soft and tender breeding,

And since you call'd me master for so long,

Here is my hand: you shall from this time be

Your master's mistress.

Olivia. 　　　　　　　　A sister! you are she.

---

1 Consider.

2 " Proper cost," i.e., personal expense.

3 Discharges.

Reënter FABIAN, *with* MALVOLIO.

Duke. Is this the madman?

Olivia.   Ay, my lord, this same.
How now, Malvolio!

Malvolio.   Madam, you have done me wrong,
Notorious wrong.

Olivia.   Have I, Malvolio? no.

Malvolio. Lady, you have.   Pray you, peruse that letter.
You must not now deny it is your hand:
Write from it, if you can, in hand or phrase;
Or say 'tis not your seal, not your invention:
You can say none of this: well, grant it then
And tell me, in the modesty of honor,
Why you have given me such clear lights of favor,
Bade me come smiling and cross-garter'd to you,
To put on yellow stockings and to frown
Upon Sir Toby and the lighter people;
And, acting this in an obedient hope,
Why have you suffer'd me to be imprison'd,
Kept in a dark house, visited by the priest,
And made the most notorious geck[1] and gull
That e'er invention play'd on? tell me why.

Olivia. Alas, Malvolio, this is not my writing,
Though, I confess, much like the character:
But out of question 'tis Maria's hand.
And now I do bethink me, it was she
First told me thou wast mad; thou cam'st in smiling,
And in such forms which here were presuppos'd
Upon thee in the letter.[2]   Prithee, be content:
This practice hath most shrewdly pass'd upon thee;[3]

---

[1] Fool.

[2] "Presuppos'd upon thee," etc., i.e., supposed you would assume on reading the letter.

[3] "This . . . thee," i.e., this trick hath been most mischievously played upon thee.

7

But when we know the grounds and authors of it,
Thou shalt be both the plaintiff and the judge
Of thine own cause.

Fabian.   Good madam, hear me speak,
And let no quarrel nor no brawl to come
Taint the condition of this present hour,
Which I have wonder'd at. In hope it shall not,
Most freely I confess, myself and Toby
Set this device against Malvolio here,
Upon some stubborn and uncourteous parts
We had conceived in him: Maria writ
The letter at Sir Toby's great importance;[1]
In recompense whereof he hath married her.
How with a sportful malice it was follow'd,
May rather pluck on laughter than revenge;
If that the injuries be justly weigh'd
That have on both sides pass'd.

Olivia. Alas, poor fool, how have they baffled thee!

Clown. Why, "some are born great, some achieve greatness
and some have greatness thrown upon them." I was one, sir,
in this interlude; one Sir Topas, sir; but that's all one. "By
the Lord, fool, I am not mad." But do you remember?
"Madam, why laugh you at such a barren rascal? an you smile
not, he's gagg'd:" and thus the whirligig of time brings in his
revenges.

Malvolio. I'll be reveng'd on the whole pack of you.. [*Exit.*

Olivia. He hath been most notoriously abus'd.

Duke. Pursue him, and entreat him to a peace:
He hath not told us of the captain yet:
When that is known and golden time convents,[2]
A solemn combination shall be made
Of our dear souls. Meantime, sweet sister,
We will not part from hence. Cesario, come;

---

1 Importunity.   2 Comes fit.

For so you shall be, while you are a man;
But when in other habits you are seen,
Orsino's mistress and his fancy's queen.

[Exeunt all, except Clown.

Clown. [*Sings*]

  When that I was and a little tiny boy,
   With hey, ho, the wind and the rain,
  A foolish thing was but a toy,
   For the rain it raineth every day.

  But when I came to man's estate,
   With hey, ho, etc.
  'Gainst knaves and thieves men shut their gate,
   For the rain, etc.

  But when I came; alas! to wive,
   With hey, ho, etc.
  By swaggering could I never thrive,
   For the rain, etc.

  But when I came unto my beds,
   With hey, ho, etc.
  With toss-pots[1] still had drunken heads,
   For the rain, etc.

  A great while ago the world begun,
   With hey, ho, etc.
  But that's all one, our play is done,
   And we'll strive to please you every day.   *[Exit.*

    [1] Drunkards.

www.ingramcontent.com/pod-product-compliance
Lightning Source LLC
Chambersburg PA
CBHW032204010726
47493CB00008BA/2827